Spicy Bites of Biryani

Spicy Bites of Biryani

....because life needs a little masala

Ashwina Garg

Srishti
PUBLISHERS & DISTRIBUTORS

Srishti Publishers & Distributors
N-16, C. R. Park
New Delhi 110 019
editorial@srishtipublishers.com

First published by
Srishti Publishers & Distributors in 2013

Typeset by EGP at Srishti

This book is dedicated to my husband, Anurag, my kids Arnav and Arushi, my mom and all my friends who have always given me the space and support to make my dreams come true.

ɔຮ

I would like to thank Srishti Publishers for having faith in my book and helping me turn my manuscript into the book it is today.

IT'S ALL ABOUT APPEARANCES

Aditi took a sip of her cappuccino and looked at Vishal sympathetically. They were sitting in a *Café Coffee Day* in Secunderabad. She didn't remember what she had told him the last time they had met, but he looked a bit desperate now.

"I understand what you're saying, Vishal. The thing is my marriage was fixed by my parents when I was eighteen years old. Now…er…Vikram is suffering from cancer so even though we don't love each other anymore, I have to stick with him." She tried to squeeze out a few tears from her eyes but they wouldn't cooperate. She settled for a sniffle.

"Who's this Vikram with cancer?" he asked suspiciously. "Last time we met, you said that you were going to the US to do your MBA because you got a full scholarship to Yale and you couldn't refuse."

Shit! So that's what she had told him. This break up was taking longer than expected. She had to attend Mayank's mom's anniversary and Jayshree is going to be very upset if she was late. "Er…that too. I'm hoping that going to Yale will help me get over you."

"I still can't understand why you can't just tell this guy that you don't love him anymore. It's not like we are living in the sixteenth century where marriages are fixed at birth," he said frustrated.

"Look, I need to go. Er...Vivek...sorry Vikram is going to have chemo today so I really need to go. I hope you can understand." She clasped his hand with both of hers and looked deeply into his eyes. "I'm so sorry!"

She was going to miss Vishal. But this had to be done. He was getting too serious for comfort. She couldn't understand why this happened all the time. Just when she was beginning to enjoy a guy's company, he started getting possessive about her. She stood up. She gave him a lingering look and dashed out of the coffee shop.

When she was safely ensconced in her car, she took a deep breath. She looked at her watch. It was 7 p.m. already. She didn't have time to go home and change. She checked her tote in the back seat. She always carried a couple of outfits and shoes in the car with her. She never knew when she would have to go from wedding to book reading in the matter of hours. She took out a dress and her high-heeled shoes from her tote and looked around the parking lot. She was alone. She peeled off her blouse and pulled the dress over her head. She lifted her hips and tried to take off her skinny jeans and pull down her dress simultaneously. She banged her knee hard on the steering wheel. Shit! That would leave a bruise. She checked her make-up in the rear view mirror. All she needed was a fresh coat of lipstick, some eye shadow, liner and mascara and she was done.

Meanwhile, Jayshree carefully applied the mauve eye shadow across her eyelids and surveyed the results in mirror. She stuck her tongue out at her image. Her mauve eyelids, rouged cheeks and bright red lips made her look like a total idiot. She rushed to the bathroom to scrub her face clean wondering what she did wrong. When Aditi had done her make-up, she had looked so gorgeous.

After emerging from the bathroom, she realized there was no time to redo the make-up, so she just patted some powder on her face from her new compact and applied some lip gloss on her lips. She stared at herself again. She didn't look glamorous, but at least she didn't look like a clown. She picked up her purse and went out into the living room, where Mayank was patiently waiting for her while watching the news on television.

"What happened to blue dress that you borrowed from Aditi," he asked knitting his brows together while Jayshree nervously smoothed the silk salwar kameez that she had put on.

"Why? Don't you think this looks good? Should I show you how the blue dress looks?" said Jayshree anxiously.

"No. No. this looks great," he said hastily. She had already tried on three outfits and if she changed again, he knew they were going to be really late.

"Let's just go before I change my clothes again. Then we'll get late and your mom will have something else to crib about."

Mayank's mother was a glamorous socialite who loved to mingle with other socialites. She was very disappointed when her studious son had refused to take over his father's transport business and pursued higher studies in the US. She was horrified when three years later he fell in love with an even more studious Jayshree and insisted on marrying her.

Today was Jayshree's in-laws wedding anniversary, and a big party had been organized at the *Grand Kakatiya*. Her in-laws never needed an excuse to throw a party. It seemed like every second day, a momentous occasion was being commemorated and her mother-in-law would summon the entire clan to Mayank's parent's monstrously large house. To be fair, the whole family was a gregarious, fun-loving crowd, but Jayshree was not a big fan of large social gatherings. Given a choice, Jayshree would be curled up in sofa somewhere with a steaming hot cup of South Indian coffee and a good book. Luckily, Mayank understood her perfectly and mostly left her to her own devices.

Her dad had warned her about how her life would be if she married Mayank, but one look at warm brown eyes, broad shoulders and razor-sharp intellect had melted all her reservations. They had met in California, where they both worked for Apache Systems. Mayank had completed his Master's degree from the prestigious Stanford University in California, while she, the total Tamilian Brahmin that she was, had graduated from IIT, Madras.

On their return to Hyderabad, at Mayank's parent's insistence, Mayank had preferred to start his own software company instead of joining his father's business and she was thankful for that. Now their software company was doing quite well, and Mayank has earned the unending love and respect of his father.

Still, Jayshree pined for her life in the States. She had loved her crazy, exciting job and her friends and she missed the weekends that they spent together hiking, camping, skiing or just hanging out at the mall. Most of all, she missed the total freedom that she experienced there. Here in India, her every minute was accounted for. When she wasn't working, she was dealing with her house or her parents or her in-laws, or

Mayank. Or their other assorted relatives. Like this party she had to attend tonight.

"Thank God Aditi's going to be there," she sighed as she thought about her friend. Crazy, whacky Aditi could make even the most mundane situation exciting. But Aditi was going to be so disappointed that she hadn't worn the aqua Raven & Rose dress that she had lent her.

"Tired?" asked Mayank as he deftly maneuvered the Audi through the traffic. "Don't worry. I told mom that we have an early-morning telephonic conference tomorrow and we won't be able to stay long. Do you remember Sanjay Bolisetti? I've invited him for the party tonight." Sanjay had been a senior in Mayank's college and had also been a Senior Manager in Apache where both Mayank and Jayshree worked when they were in the Bay Area. "Sanjay left Apache to start Paradigm Networks. It went public three years ago and got bought over by SAP for millions of dollars. Lucky, huh?"

"He was that tall, nerdy guy who practically lived in the office, right?" replied Jayshree, thinking back about their life in Fremont, California.

"Yeah. But he's not so nerdy anymore. It amazing how fast a few million dollars can turn a nerd into a sophisticated guy," drawled Mayank. "He wants to get married and is in two minds about settling down in Hyderabad, so I'm trying to convince him."

"Isn't he quite old now? I thought he was going around with Sheetal? What happened?" asked Jayshree, but Mayank wasn't listening. He had stopped the car and rolled down the window to curse at an auto driver who had rear-ended his car. Jayshree rolled her eyes.

Soon the huge gates of the *Kakatiya* approached. She gathered up the lovely *Ganesha* statue that she had bought for her in-laws. She perked up considerably since hearing about Sanjay. It was always nice to meet people from their old life.

WINE AND WHINING

"**O**h Mayank! *Kahan the tum log?* We were waiting just for you. *Itne late ho!*" exclaimed his mother as they entered the hall. Dolly Arora hugged him tight. She was wearing black velvet stretch pants with a heavily embroidered *kurti* and was enveloped in a fragrant cloud of Sarah Jessica Parker's Lovely perfume. She turned to Jayshree, noting her simple *salwar kameez*. "How are you, Jayshree? That *salwar kameez* really suits your simple looks! Come both of you. Meet everybody!"

At that same minute, Aditi was walking across the lobby towards the opened doors of elevator balancing precariously on 4-inch black Jimmy Choos. Several heads turned towards her as she made her way across the slippery, black granite floors and into the waiting elevator. She heaved a sigh of relief as the elevator doors shut while she was safely inside it. Smoothing her Gauri and Nainika outfit, she quickly thanked the kind soul who had held the doors open for her. She glanced around the elevator to check out the other people in the elevator. She liked to observe people because it helped her to develop the characters of the books that she wrote. A man in crisp white shirt, Armani slacks and shiny, black shoes was typing furiously into his iPhone. His fingers were long and quick. She was fascinated. She had never met anybody who could type so fast on a touch screen before. It was magical.

"Which floor? We're all waiting," enquired Mr Fast-typer impatiently looking up from his iPhone. Aditi smiled self-consciously as she punched the button for the basement. She wanted to say something curt to Mr Fast-typer but the elevator doors opened and she quickly made her way to the hall where the Arora's were celebrating their anniversary.

As soon as she entered the hall, her eyes scanned the room for a familiar face. They rested on Jayshree, who was standing forlornly with Anu *mami* and several other relatives of Mayank. Anu *mami* was talking animatedly to Jayshree, who looked like a deer caught in the jaws of a lioness. Aditi quickly made her way to Jayshree.

"Why didn't you wear the dress I loaned you? What did Dolly aunty think about your outfit?" she whispered giving Jayshree a hug.

"She thought it suited my plain looks," replied Jayshree, happy that Aditi had now made an appearance. "I was wondering when you planned to come. I've just got a long lecture about how motherhood will change my life. Anu *mami* was just explaining the entire process of in-vitro fertilization to me. I wonder why she doesn't explain it to Mayank. I'd like to see his face when she does."

"It's just small talk, Babe. No need to be so hassled. Chill, okay?" said Aditi as she summoned a nearby waiter and plucked two champagne glasses from him. "Here, drink this and watch me." She turned to Anu *mami*. "Have you lost weight, Anu *mami*? You look so fabulous in that green chiffon. It brings out the highlights in your hair. Those two waiters over there can't get their eyes off you."

Anu *mami* turned a deep red and eyed the two waiters who were busy serving sparkling white wine to the guests. She giggled and patted her hair. "*Arre*, Thanks, *beti*. Yesterday only I had a facial and colour. I was just wondering how it looks." She preened unselfconsciously.

Jayshree and Aditi looked at each other and laughed. She took the glass from Aditi and debated if she should really drink it. It either made her sleepy or giggly and she didn't want to be afflicted by either condition when she was with her mother-in-law. On the other hand, it would probably make the party more bearable, she thought. "Cheers. And please don't call me Babe," retorted Jayshree.

"Okay, Babe," came the cheeky reply.

"Hi," said Mayank who appeared at their side with Aditi's Mr Fast-typer in tow. "Ladies, let me introduce you to Sanjay Bolisetti. I'm trying to convince him to move to Hyderabad, so please be on your best behaviour. Especially you Aditi."

"Why especially me? Am I a bad girl? Hi. I'm Aditi Patil," said Aditi, introducing herself. Mr Fast-typer certainly looked friendlier now. Maybe he broke the fast-typing-on-a-touch-screen world record.

"Let's just say that you're you," retorted Mayank. Mayank and Aditi were family friends. Aditi had been a great help when Mayank and Jayshree had moved back to Hyderabad. She had immediately befriended Jayshree and taken her furniture shopping, when she realized that both Mayank and Jayshree were completely hopeless at it. She had even taught Jayshree to drive a stick shift when it appeared that Mayank might murder his pretty wife while trying to teach her to drive in the chaotic Hyderabadi traffic.

"Hi. I think we met in the elevator. I've heard a lot about you from Mayank. He says you're a writer. That's really interesting," said Sanjay politely.

"How come you're thinking about moving to India now, Sanjay," said Jayshree. "I thought you loved the US?"

"Well....India has changed a lot now. Anyway I needed a change. I want to get married and settle down. Somehow that's not happening in the US."

"Why are guys so desperate to get married nowadays?" exclaimed Aditi. "Can't you just tell your mom that you can do your own cooking and cleaning?" she asked, snatching another glass of wine.

There was an awkward silence. "Actually, my parents are no more," replied Sanjay quietly. "So... what kind of books do you write? I hear you're quite a celebrity," he asked quickly. He didn't want to discuss either his parents or his marriage plans in front of a total stranger.

"She's a writer of romance novels. She wrote two bestsellers *The Gulmohar Tree* and *East Meets West,*" replied Jayshree beginning to feel the effects of the champagne. She wondered why she had dreaded this party so much this morning. She was having so much fun now.

"Really?" replied Sanjay, deftly intercepting a waiter and hijacking a plate of *kebabs* and a plate of spring rolls. "A romance writer who thinks marriage is about cooking and cleaning? Isn't it difficult for you to write about love?"

"No. That's how most guys think about marriage," spluttered Aditi loudly. "Writing comes from my imagination.

Do I have to murder somebody to write a murder mystery?" she said getting agitated.

"Why don't you try a *kebab*, Aditi?" said Mayank soothingly.

"I'm sorry. I didn't mean to upset you. You're probably a great writer. I haven't really read any of your books," replied Sanjay ruefully. "Look, let's have some dinner. The buffet looks fabulous. Now where are those Single Malts you promised, Mayank? All I can see is this cheap stuff."

"I'm sorry too, about that remark about your mom, but what I said is perfectly true. It happens all the time," mumbled Aditi, still angry. "Stop looking at me, Mayank. I'm not drunk. You should worry about Shree. She looks tipsy."

Three pairs of eyes turned to look at Jayshree, who was grinning goofily. "You're such a bad influence on my wife, Aditi. How much has she had to drink?" Mayank asked Aditi as he reached out for Jayshree hand. "Are you okay?" he asked amused, patting Jayshree's hand gently and tucking it in the crook of his arm.

"Ammam. Kavalai padaathey! Mayank, Enakku pasi. Hey! We should go dancing now, Mayank." She paused and looked deeply into his eyes. "Mayank, Naan annai virumpukiren," she said soulfully.

He tightened his grip on her arm. "Ya. I love you too," he replied gravely. "Why don't you two carry on and get to know each other. We were going to leave early anyway. We have a busy day tomorrow."

"Come home for lunch this weekend, Sanjay. We can show you how wonderful Hyderabad is and we could drink those Single Malts I promised you," said Mayank before walking towards his parents to tell them they were leaving.

"So tell me how you became a writer," said Sanjay turning to Aditi and leading her to the buffet table. "How do you create the characters?"

Aditi was just about to reply when she saw Ayush near the buffet table. Ayush was her old boyfriend and she was constantly bumping into him all over the place. They had got along really well till he had decided that they should wait till they got married to sleep together. She had dumped him the next day. What kind of guy refused a girl when she had offered herself willingly? He had to be a wuss. Or impotent. She didn't tell him that was the reason for their break up, of course. She was more tactful than that. She had told him that her aunt had died and that she was too upset to be in a relationship.

She desperately looked for a place to hide. Meeting him would only necessitate more lies. She didn't like lying but sometimes it seemed like the only way out. Anyway, they weren't the type of lies that hurt anybody. They were just stories that she made up in her head to make life easier. She was a writer after all. Fiction came easily to her.

"Could you just stand here in front of me?" she asked Sanjay.

"Why?" he asked nonplussed.

"Because I want to paint you," she replied tersely. "What do you think? Old boyfriend."

"Is he giving you problems? Should I call security?" he asked troubled.

"No, *re*. I'm just using you as a wall. I don't want him to see me and get emotional again. That can get so tedious after a while," she explained.

"Very tedious," he agreed with straight face. It was easier just to agree with everything she said. "So what went wrong?"

She sighed and looked at him. Nobody really understood her way of thinking. Her mother had been so angry that she had dumped a great guy like Ayush. Maybe a stranger would understand. "He was saving himself for marriage. Can you believe that? In this day and age." She still found it hard to digest.

"Terrible crime," he replied with false sympathy. So sexy. It was a pity she was such a whack job, he thought regretfully. "So, has he gone? Can we go for dinner?"

"No. Thanks. I see some friends that I want to meet. See you sometime," she said brightly before making her way to another group of friends and leaving Sanjay standing all alone in the middle of the crowded hall.

BONDING OVER BRUNCH

*I*t was almost noon, but Sanjay was still lying lazily in bed reading Ms Loveleen's Blog. A friend of his had forwarded one of her articles to him and he had become hooked. The writer had a deep insight into love and a droll sense of humour which he liked. She was pretty active on the forums too.... giving advice, passing witty comments and sometimes seriously counselling anyone who needed help, making the website entertaining, yet effective. She always discussed some tiny, yet interesting facet of love that made a person think about their relationships and their life a little more deeply. He smiled as he finished reading her latest blog on who should pay for the first date and then checked the time. It was almost time for him to go to Mayank's house for lunch. He added his own comments to her blog and got up to get ready.

Meanwhile, Mayank and Aditi were busy helping Jayshree make lunch that Sunday. Actually, Mayank and Jayshree were making lunch while Aditi was the official taster of the day. She tottered around the kitchen in her red Steve Madden shoes taking little bites of everything.

"You really think showing Sanjay the Charminar is going to

14

make him want to move to Hyderabad, Mickey?" Aditi asked Mayank, while popping a cashew into her mouth.

"No. But I'm sure if he takes one look at you, he'll stay," he said eyeing her low cut blouse and skin tight Rockstar jeans. "And don't call me Mickey. You know I hate it."

"Stop it you two. Sanjay has already seen the Charminar and he's already decided to move to Hyderabad. So shush. I can't cook when there's tension. Let's have lunch and then we can decide what to do," said Jayshree crossly as she burnt the garlic.

"You better not do anything to him," Mayank said to Aditi.

"What am I going to do to him?" she asked confused.

"I don't know. Whatever the hell you do to make guys like you. He's not your type," he muttered, remembering his college days. He had had a massive crush on her, but she had been gloriously oblivious.

"What's my type? And who are you to tell me what to do?" she said outraged.

"Children. Children," chided Jayshree.

Both Jayshree and Mayank were very good cooks and they liked having small groups of their friends over for a meal over the weekend. Today Jayshree had invited Aditi and Sanjay over for lunch and was busy bustling about the kitchen making a vegetable *biryani*, a *paneer* curry and *naans*, while Mayank was making his famous chicken curry and fried prawns.

"You do know that in India you can always hire people to do the cooking for you," drawled Aditi watching Jayshree sweat over the hot stove while popping another cashew in her mouth. "Why is it that even when a woman has a career, she is still in charge of this menial housework after marriage? That's another reason I don't want to get married. No man is going to tell me what to do or not do."

"Don't start. I'm not in the mood," said Jayshree adding onions. "And don't eat all those cashews, I need it later. Why don't you be a dear and set the table. The crockery is in the cupboards near the dining table. And don't be rude with Sanjay, please. Let's just enjoy each other's company."

"Okay, Okay. Guys like that really irritate me. They remind me of Rajesh. They think they are so fantastic they want everybody to treat them like Gods," said Aditi morosely. "My parent's would kill to get me married to a guy like that."

"So what's wrong with that? Don't you want find somebody to spend the rest of your life with? Sanjay is a really nice guy. You could do much worse," said Jayshree. She sighed inwardly. They had this conversation at least once every week. Sometimes she felt like she was a parent and Aditi, a recalcitrant child.

Not that Aditi really needed any extra parenting. Her parents were both doctors and extremely interested in every aspect of her life. Her father was a famous orthopaedic surgeon and her mother was a gynaecologist. Both were extremely unhappy by her choice of profession. Aditi was a writer who had written two books, but Aditi parents thought that writing was a hobby, not a real career. When they realized that they couldn't influence her career choices, they shifted their attention to her choice of husband. Aditi managed to thwart those plans as well by declaring that she would never get married and having a string of casual boyfriends. As far as she knew, she was living the perfect life and she didn't need anybody to ruin it for her.

"Shree, I can't live my life according to somebody else's likes and dislikes. I mean look at you. You're pretty, intelligent, financially independent but you always do exactly what Mayank tells you to do. Don't you get bored?" asked Aditi.

Jayshree felt silent. Is that how she appeared to others? A shadow of a woman who only did what her husband expected her to do. Well, it certainly wasn't true. It was just her Tamilian reticence meeting Mayank's Punjabi aggressiveness. At the end of the day, Mayank was always protective of her and had her best interests at heart. Maybe she had made more compromises in their marriage than he had, but wasn't that true of all Indian marriages? "He kills cockroaches and drives away the lizards," murmured Jayshree defending Mayank.

"That's not the only problem. They only bother to be romantic and sensitive till you sleep with them. After that they go back to being their selfish, boorish selves," said Aditi warming up to her favourite topic.

"Not all guys are like that. When you find that special guy, it'll be different," promised Jayshree absent-mindedly. She was still thinking about all the advantages of being married to Mayank. He was cute, had strong arms and was good in bed. On the more prosaic side, he was successful, well-educated and intelligent. All in all a pretty good deal, she thought grudgingly. But he did manage to get his own way most of the time....

"It won't be different. They just fool you into thinking that it'll be different. Once you sleep with them, they take you totally for granted. If the guy wants to get married, you will. If he doesn't, you won't. I'm not going to let anybody have that much control over my life," said Aditi more to herself than to Jayshree.

"Hello! I'm still in the room. Do either of you care?" asked Mayank amused.

"I don't always do what you want me to do. I don't," said Jayshree to Mayank adamantly. Her jaw was beginning to jut out in the dangerous way it did when she was getting ready for battle.

The doorbell rang and Mayank ran to open it. "I think that's my cue to exit," he said gratefully. "I'm going to get you for this," he warned Aditi wagging his finger at her before leaving to open the door.

Aditi rose to set the table, just as Sanjay walked through the door. He was carrying a huge bouquet of flowers and a duty-free bag full of goodies. He looked smart in a red polo T-shirt and faded blue jeans. His hair looked damp like he had just showered and he smelt good too. *F from Ferragamo*, if she wasn't mistaken. She had a weakness for men who dressed well, smelt good and had good manners. And Sanjay had great hands too. So ten out of ten for him. If he ever asks me out, I might accept, she thought wickedly to herself. Especially since Mayank had warned her to stay away. Like he was a little lamb and she was the wolf.

"Flowers for the beautiful…,"declared Sanjay as presented the huge bunch of pink carnations and lilies to Aditi. "And a bag of goodies for the …uh…um…good," he said as he handed the bag to Jayshree.

"That's okay, Sanjay. I haven't received any compliments from a man for ages now. I'm kinda used to it," said Jayshree, who had come into the living room to greet Sanjay. She shot a meaningful look at her husband.

"Ohh…Trouble in paradise," said Sanjay smirking as he sank into the brown sofa next to Mayank and patted his knee.

"It's all Aditi's fault," grumbled Mayank. "She going to get us divorced one day."

Jayshree peeked into the bag and saw two bottles of wine, a huge box of Godiva chocolates, a bottle of expensive perfume and several assorted cheeses. "Thanks for all this stuff, Sanjay. It's so sweet of you. I really miss this stuff here. Even when you can find it, it's hideously expensive. Is this wine from the Napa Valley? God I really miss California."

"So what have you been up to? Saw any houses that you liked?" enquired Mayank while keeping the wine in the fridge to cool.

"Some of the gated communities are good, but they are really far from the main city. I'm still thinking about what to do. Your mother called too. She's very keen to invite me for dinner."

"She probably has some hidden agenda, somewhere. Some girl she wants to marry off," said Mayank.

"Yeah! All my far off relatives with girls to marry off are all coming out of the woodwork too. This is why I sometimes think about moving to Bombay. I don't know anyone there!" he joked half-seriously.

Sanjay was confused about what to do with his life. Looking at couples like Mayank and Jayshree made him want to get married too. He had tried his hand at love with Sheetal, who had been his colleague in Apache Networks and Paradigm, but they had broken up. Now, after his company had been acquired by SAP, there were plenty of women who were interested in him but he could never be sure if a woman liked him or his money. He had come to India to clear his head. Just thirty five and already suffering a mid-life crisis, he thought ruefully.

He had rented a flat and bought himself a BMW trying to figure out whether he permanently wanted to settle down in

Hyderabad or not. He had casually mentioned to his aunt that he was interested in getting married and a horde of proposals had come his way. A rich bachelor without parents had brought out the mothering instinct in all the aunties that knew him. Ever since he had arrived in Hyderabad, he had been inundated with invitations to lunches, dinners, weddings, engagements and house warming ceremonies and he even enjoyed it sometimes. But it wasn't the same as having someone of your own to come home to at the end of the day.

"Do you want to go around Hyderabad or do you want to watch the India-Australia match on TV?" asked Mayank after they had cleared the plates and Aditi brought out a huge strawberry cheesecake and cut out big chunks of it for everybody.

"Dude, I couldn't eat another bite. Let's watch the match. I don't think I can move," said Sanjay happily.

Aditi handed Sanjay a plate of cheesecake. "You know if you want to see some houses and apartments, I can show you around. A friend of mine bought a flat in a nice complex in Kondapur. There are some really nice duplex and townhouses still available there. I could show it to you if you like." Aditi cursed herself. Showing him an apartment complex sounded so lame. But she didn't want to be openly flirtatious. Mayank would kill her.

He looked at her coolly. She had been pretty well-behaved today. No outbursts or outrageous comments. What did he have to lose? "That would be great. Are you free tomorrow? I could pick you up at your house and go see this place," replied Sanjay.

"Fine. I'm busy in the morning but we could go after lunch," she said nonchalantly, ignoring Mayank's frown.

"Hmm...Why don't we have lunch together and then we can go see this place. If that's okay with you," said Sanjay. She looked pretty good in those jeans. A little female company never hurt anybody, he told himself.

"Great," said Aditi brightly.

Later, Sanjay and Mayank lay sprawled on the sofa, while Aditi and Jayshree moved to the bedroom to gossip some more. One hour into the cricket match, just when Virat Kohli was getting into perfect form by hitting two sixes, the electricity went and the television turned dark.

"Shoot!" cursed Mayank and turned to Sanjay. "You wanted to experience India. This is it. Heaven and hell... all rolled into one!" The party ended quickly after that.

HOUSE-HUNTING IN HYDERABAD

*T*he next day, Aditi was busy writing. At least she was making an effort to write. She stared at her laptop. Her heroine was in great distress because her friend Maya had just told her that the man she loved had lied to her about his past after sleeping with her. Aditi tried to get into the mood of the scene by imagining herself as the heroine. She just couldn't. "You poor thing," she muttered to her heroine Tara, "My head is so screwed up. I'm not able to imagine any kind of future for you."

Aditi turned on her iPod. Music sometimes helped her write. She stared at the screen and the blinking cursor stared back at her accusingly. She re-read the chapter she had written and groaned. She buried her head in hands. Aditi Patil, writer of two sensitively-written, critically-acclaimed novels, was turning into a soft-porn writer. Her editor had advised her to spice up her latest novel with some more intimate scenes, but she was having a hard time finding the fine line between sensual and vulgar. Maybe she was giving too much importance to her love life lately and not enough to her career. The thought that she didn't have a book in her anymore was starting to keep her awake at nights. Sometimes she wondered if her father was right after all. She was no writer.

Suddenly her mobile buzzed and she got back into the real world. She checked her cell phone and her heart skipped a beat when she realized that it was a message from Sanjay.

"Will be at your place by 12:30. Hope that's ok," it said.

"Shit," she cursed. She hadn't even had a bath yet and it was already 11:30. She had been so engrossed in her writing. Or her non-writing, she admitted ruefully. She perked up when she thought of Sanjay. Maybe there was a story in Sanjay's life somewhere.

"Sure. Great. See you then. Bye," she typed back and dashed to the bathroom. She rushed back out and pulled out all her clothes from her cupboard. "Jeans…Jeans...I need jeans. Blouses… Blouses. What to wear?" She took out her white *chikan kurti* and held it against her and watched herself in the mirror.

"Maybe simple is the way to go today." She placed her clothes on the bed and rushed into the bathroom to take a bath. She showered at record speed and was blow-drying her hair by 12:15. She put on several silver bangles and her silver dangling earrings and applied *kajal* under her eyes. She looked at herself in the mirror. She looked great.

"Whew. Almost didn't make it," she said as she plunked herself on the couch. Her mother was having lunch of *aloo parathas* and curd. She was a mild-mannered, gentle lady living with a dominating, opinionated husband and a stubborn daughter. She was convinced that if she didn't have a career, she would have completely lost her mind in her household.

"Do you want some lunch? It looks like you're going out," she asked her daughter.

"Yes. I'm taking Mayank's friend, Sanjay, to see a few houses in Kondapur."

"Is he the boy that Dolly aunty was talking about at her anniversary party?" asked her mother brightening up. "It's nice that you are taking the time to show him around. Everybody is saying what a nice, simple boy he is."

"Why is every unmarried man called a boy irrespective of how old he is?" snorted Aditi looking at her watch. "Anyway, don't get any ideas. He's not my type. I don't like these US-returned guys." 12:45.Where was he?

"I don't think any boy is exactly your type," replied her mother.

Finally the bell rang. Aditi rushed to open the door. Sanjay stood outside. "You're late. Don't you think other people's time is valuable?"

"Aditi, let him come in first," said her mother exasperated. "So sorry. Sometimes I don't know what's wrong with this girl. Come in please. It was nice of you to come. Will you have some tea or coffee?"

"We're going out to lunch, *Aai*. Why would he have some tea or coffee at lunch time?" said Aditi irritated.

"Is that how you talk to your mother all the time?" asked Sanjay horrified. "No Aunty. Not today, thanks. Why don't you join us for lunch?" Sanjay asked Aditi's mother politely.

"Not today. You children go and enjoy yourself," said Aditi's mother.

"You really know how to charm all the aunties, don't you? I was beginning to feel like I was in some kind of soap where the mother was reunited with her long lost son," said Aditi when both of them walked to the car. Sanjay opened the door for Aditi and then got into the car himself. Aditi was enchanted. Nobody had opened a door for her since she was a kid.

"Why are you always so rude?" said Sanjay angrily. "What have I done to annoy you? I know I was a bit impatient with you in the elevator the first time we met, but is that really such a big deal? I really like Jayshree and Mayank and I know that you are close to them so I'm trying to be friendly, but I get nothing from your end. I just want to fit in here and settle down. What's wrong with that?"

Aditi was silent for a while. "You remind me of a guy I was engaged to when I was younger. His name was Rajesh. He came down from the US for two weeks to get married. His parents wanted to have this fancy four-day long wedding in a five star setting with lot of gold and expensive gifts for all their relatives, all at my parent's expense, of course. They treated my parents like crap. Then one day before the wedding his dad asked my dad when he was going to transfer the plot he owned in Jubilee Hills to his son. We'd known this guy only for a week! I broke off the engagement and decided to concentrate on my career and never get married ever. It makes me really angry that my parents and I had to go through that. I don't understand how people can just come to India for a week or two and then get married after barely knowing each other."

"Oh!" said Sanjay, staring through the windscreen for a few minutes. "I wasn't expecting that. But not all guys who come to India to get married are like that. Most of them just want to find a decent girl and live happily ever after. And by the way, I'm really offended that I remind you of him. I haven't asked your dad for his property yet."

Aditi laughed. "I don't know. It's just some superficial resemblance and because you've come back to India specifically to get married. I mean, aren't there thousands of Indian girls in the US. Didn't you like any of them? Someone like you would find anyone. Why do you want to marry a stranger?"

Sanjay thought before answering. "I lost my mother when I was thirteen and my father when I was twenty. I don't have any brothers or sisters. Even Mayank and I weren't very close in the US even though we went to college together. I've been on my own for fourteen years. Longer actually, but that a totally different story. I'm beginning to crave some drama in my life." He fell silent and rubbed his neck absent-mindedly. "Look, I think we started off on the wrong foot. So can we be friends now? You're not going to give me any trouble?" asked Sanjay.

She smiled. "Okay. Let's be friends. In fact, since you're so desperate to get married, I'm going to set you up with some of my eligible, single friends. You can be sure that anyone that I set you up with will be really good marriage material."

"Please don't. There are enough of people already doing that," he joked.

"I'm serious. I can think of two people right this minute. I think I'll call Sujaya right now," she said taking out her phone.

"Are you insane? Give me that!" he tried to snatch the phone out of her hand, but she quickly got out of the car and dialled. She spoke on her phone for a few minutes before getting inside the car again.

"Well, it's all set for tonight. Sujaya is so gorgeous that you'll thank me for the rest of your life. Am I great person to know or what?"

"You're a crazy person. I'm not going out with any Sujaya. Now tell me where you want to go for lunch. There's a nice Chinese place just down this road."

After lunch, Aditi and Sanjay drove down to 'Belle Vista' where her friend's apartment was located. Aditi had to admit, it had been quite pleasant talking to him during lunch. She couldn't remember a time when she felt so comfortable with somebody. If she wasn't so anti-marriage, she wouldn't mind applying for the post of his wife herself. She didn't think she would have to try too hard. He looked happy to be with her.

They entered the elegant gates of the gated community and went over to the manager's office. A thin, bespectacled man looked up at them.

"Hello Vignesh. This is my friend Mr Sanjay. He was interested in seeing the townhouses from the inside. Is it possible today?" asked Aditi.

"Yes. Yes. Welcome Sir. I'm Vignesh, Sir," he said beaming and rushed to shake Sanjay's hand. "Hello Madam! Welcome to our wonderful Belle Vista Living Solutions. You must be from America, no? I can recognize when people are from America. We have many people from America living here. You will not have any problem. Everything is best quality, Sir, just like America." He opened a drawer and handed them brochures of the houses. "We have many famous people also living here. Recently only, Sudhir Reddy has bought one of our duplex apartments for Sulochana. Do you know Sulochana, very big Telugu actress? She goes to the gym everyday at six o'clock," he said conspiratorially like it was the biggest feature of the complex.

"Sudhir Reddy? The founder of Biochem Labs? Isn't he married with grownup kids?" Sanjay asked Aditi surprised.

"Like that has ever stopped anybody," said Aditi drily. "Don't worry. You too can afford to set up a couple of starlets for yourself now that you're in Hyderabad." She wiggled her eyebrows suggestively. He looked at her like she had lost her mind.

Vignesh drew their attention back to the features of Belle Vista. "We have many special services here... house-keeping services, coaches, full-service spa, doctor, nutritionist, fitness-instructor, life coach... everything. All the details are in the brochure."

"Life coach? What does a life coach do?" Sanjay asked.

"She's a therapist for people with high stress, Sir. She gives advice about how to reduce stress in your life. She also practices past-life regression, Tarot, Reiki, everything to make your life good," said Vignesh cheerfully. "Now we'll see the model houses. Come." He opened the door and held it open for them.

Hyderabad has changed a lot since I was here last," muttered Sanjay as they walked through the beautifully manicured lawns towards the townhouses. Vignesh opened the door of the model house.

"See I want to show you something special?" he said and clapped his hands once. The lights turned on. "Now see, ok?" He clapped twice and the curtains closed. "These are our special sound-activated switches. They can be installed in any of the houses. Special for our high-tech residents. See now again, ok?" He clapped thrice and water started flowing from a fountain in the corner. He clapped thrice again and the water fountain stopped.

Just then his phone started ringing. "Just one moment, please. Please sit. I have some urgent work. You can see the house. I'll come back in five minutes," he said and left.

The moment he was gone, Aditi turned to Sanjay. "Isn't this place a total chick magnet," she said excitedly and clapped. The lights turned off and it turned pitch dark.

"Turn on the lights. It's too dark. Why would anybody put such thick curtains in a model house? Shit!" he said as he stumbled into a potted plant. Both of them clapped simultaneously. The water fountain near Aditi started to flow. She yelled and bumped into a pedestal with a statue of a warrior with a spear. Both desperately started clapping again. Nothing happened.

"Wait. It only works when one person claps, okay," he said.

"Oh! You know everything, don't you? This place is creepy. Eek! What was that?" she yelped. Somehow Sanjay had managed to open the curtains and light streamed in from the window. He found Aditi fighting with the curtains at the other end of the room.

"You just said it was a chick magnet," he said, putting the potted plant back in its place.

"I just changed my mind. Shit!" she cursed. The warrior's spear had fallen and pierced a cushion. She placed the warrior back on his pedestal and plucked the cushion from his spear.

"What do I do with this?" she asked looking at the torn cushion.

"So, now you want me to be in charge?" he retorted. Aditi still looked dazed from her battle with the curtains. He gently took it from her and placed the cushion under the other cushions. "Let's get the hell out of here!"

Aditi ran after him. "Are we really going to do this?" she asked horrified.

"Yup!" he replied. They walked briskly till they left the

townhouses behind. When they both came near a park bench, they both sat down and started laughing.

"I can't believe we did that. I have so many friends in this complex. Everybody knows me here!" she wailed and then started laughing again. She became introspective after a while. "I wanted to buy an apartment here too, but my parents won't let me move out of the house till I'm married. I don't know when I'll have my own house. Can you believe it? I'm thirty two years old and still ruled by my parents."

"You can afford to buy your own house? I'm impressed. I didn't know writers make so much money," said Sanjay.

"They don't! Not in India. I started working in an ad agency when I was eighteen because I didn't want to study…much to my parent's dismay. I worked as a copywriter in Dubai for four years. I saved up quite a bit and my dad invested the money for me," she said smiling. "So where are you taking Sujaya tonight?"

"I'm not going out with any Sujaya," he said firmly. He was not into blind dates. He didn't want to be with an unknown female and pretend to like her. Tomorrow when all this crazy blind date business was over, he was going to register himself on a matrimonial website and seriously search for a wife. But tonight…he had to get through tonight. He had an idea. "Why don't you join us?"

"Are you mad? What'll I do with the two of you? It's a date. Take her to the *Westin*. She likes that place," she said happily. Aditi liked setting people up. Sometimes she felt inspired to write by watching other people together. "And by the way, Sujaya is a very innocent, kind and sweet girl who has been protected all her life. Don't try anything funny, Sunny," she warned, punching him in the arm.

"You don't have to warn me," he protested, rubbing his arm. "And who's Sunny?"

"Sunny, short for Sanjay," she explained.

Sanjay's eyes narrowed. "Do I look like a Sunny, Aditi?" he asked coolly. He took out his phone and began to check his emails. It was bad enough that she had stooped to setting him up on a blind date, now she had the nerve to call him Sunny like he was some chubby-cheeked toddler. From CEO to this. What the hell was he doing?

Aditi smothered a smile. He was sulking. She would have been annoyed if he didn't look so cute. She felt like kissing his drooping lips to make him feel better. He was obviously used to people fawning over him and taking him seriously. She wondered if he would be interested in a little fling before he got married. "No," she said meekly. He certainly didn't look like a Sunny. "Would you prefer I call you Mr Bollisetti? Yes Sir, Mr Bolisetti. No Sir, Mr Bolisetti."

"Only if you're planning on working for me," he said, amusement lightening his eyes. His sense of humour was back.

Aditi breath caught. If only he knew what kind of work she wanted to do for him. She could imagine it now, the two of them rolling around in white sheets, getting sweaty and bonking each other brains out. But pouty lips wanted to get married. She didn't even want to imagine what married sex must look like, never mind indulge in it. "Don't be so desperate," she scolded herself without realizing that she had uttered the words aloud. There was going to be no bonking between them.

"I'm not desperate," he said scandalized. "I'm focussed on finding the right wife for me. What's wrong with that?"

"Nothing," said Aditi looking at him with mild regret. If he wanted to find a wife, let him find a wife. She didn't want to be anybody's wife. She had things she wanted to do with her life.

ALL THAT GLITTERS IS NOT GOLD

Sanjay was sitting in the lobby of the *Westin* waiting for Sujaya to turn up. He checked Ms Loveleen's Blog on his cell to see if she had replied to his comment. She had.

"You're either very conservative or very rich," said the comment. "With the raging inflation, a woman's love for shopping and men and women both working and getting equal pay, any guy who thinks that the only way to express love is through his wallet is going to wind up broke. If you're in a relationship with somebody right now, I suggest that you just exercise those vocal chords and tell her that you love her. It's significantly cheaper. Unless you're dumb. Literally and figuratively."

Sanjay laughed. His phone buzzed again. It was Sujaya. She was calling to tell him that she had arrived and that she was about to enter the lobby. Sanjay got up nervously and waited for her to step in. A tall, beautiful girl with long brown hair entered. She was wearing a pink *churidar kurta* and high heels. Sanjay walked up to the girl to introduce himself.

"Hi. I'm Sanjay. You must be Sujaya." Sujaya smiled at

him. Aditi was right. She really was gorgeous. He led her into 'Kangan', the Indian restaurant in *Westin*.

After they were seated, Sujaya turned to Sanjay. "Hi. I've heard so much about you from Aditi. She was my senior in school, but we became friends because my parents and her parents were both in the Rotary together."

"Aditi praised you a lot too." he said and called the waiter. "Shall we order?"

She looked at the menu. "I'm a vegetarian. My Guruji advised me to stop eating non-vegetarian food, fried food and all processed foods so I don't eat it anymore. What about you?"

"I eat anything that tastes good. But it's good that you eat healthy. It really works for you. You're really beautiful," he said gallantly.

"Thanks," she said politely. She assessed him secretly from behind her menu. He was good-looking but older than her. She wondered what Aditi was thinking setting her up with him. She usually never went on dates. Her parents were too conservative. Aditi had done a lot of creative lying to get her out of the house tonight.

"So what do you do?" Sanjay asked her. The waiter had brought an assortment of papads, pickles and crunchies for them to munch on while they decided on their drinks. He broke off a piece of papad and popped it into his mouth. He hated this. Making meaningless conversation and trying to break the ice were not his strengths. He just wanted to get married so he could get on with the rest of his life. It was the main reason he was attracted to the concept of an arranged marriage. Delegate the unpleasant work. That was the key. Why waste energy on meaningless flattery and unnecessary emotion?

"I teach yoga. I have my own yoga studio. When I was in college, I started learning yoga as a hobby. But by the time I graduated I was really good at it, so my mother's friends asked me to teach them," she said nervously. She looked up at him. He didn't look too interested in her yoga studio but she didn't know what else to talk about.

"That's good. You're self-employed. So am I." he said smiling. The words sounded hollow even to him. He didn't think he had anything in common with Sujaya. Still, Sujaya was beautiful and physical attraction was an important part of married life. He should keep an open mind.

She relaxed a little when he smiled. "Yeah. We have so much in common," she said delighted.

"Do you see anything you like? How about broccoli? That's healthy, right? How does *tandoori* broccoli sound?" he asked surveying the menu. He motioned to the waiter and ordered the snacks. "Some wine? They have a nice Kosta Browne Pinot Noir from 2009." He looked up at her questioningly.

"Oh. No. I don't drink. Guruji is totally against drinking alcohol. He says that waking up at dawn and doing *Suryanamaskars* and *Pranayama* is more relaxing that having alcohol. You should try it. Why don't you come to my class?" she asked brightly.

Sanjay smiled at her uncertainly. He wasn't really interested in getting up at dawn to do *Suryanamaskars*. He asked for two fresh lime sodas and waited for the waiter to leave. "Maybe someday," he mumbled vaguely. The couple next to them were in a celebratory mood and had ordered a white wine. Sanjay looked at it longingly. It was the Reveilo Chardonnay Reserve that he had been meaning to check out. He had heard that it was one of the best white wines in India. He turned his attention back to Sujaya. "What are you looking for in a husband, Sujaya?"

Sujaya blushed a deep crimson. "Actually, Aditi told me, there's this guy who wants to get married, do you want to meet him? So I just said okay." She looked up at him innocently. The waiter brought their snacks and drinks. She took a sip of her soda and delicately speared a piece of broccoli and put it in her mouth.

Sanjay understood why Aditi had been so protective of her. He lifted the menu again. "So do you want to order the main course?"

"Oh no! I'm finished. I'm on this diet, you know? You're only supposed to have six small meals instead of three big ones. So this is enough for me," she said politely.

He frowned. "Are you sure?"

"Yes. Anyway, I don't have proteins and vegetables in the same meal and I don't have carbs at night," she announced virtuously.

Sanjay's fingers itched to pick his phone and start browsing the net. The US markets would have opened by now, he thought wistfully. "Doesn't it get hard to remember what to eat and what not to eat?" he asked, not the least bit interested. A waiter got a huge tray laden with food to the table next to them. He wished he could join them. He wondered if it would be rude for him to order a main course if Sujaya wasn't going to eat anything. He had no idea of correct dating etiquette and Aditi had not mentioned her friend's weird eating habits. "Coffee?" he asked in a burst of inspiration. "Would you like some?"

"Oh no! Coffee is like, full of caffeine. You know my Guruji…."

"I know. He told you not to have any," said Sanjay sadly. He didn't think he could spend the rest of his life with someone who didn't enjoy food. From Hyderabadi *biryani* to juicy American burgers, from Italian *spaghetti alla puttanesca* to Greek *moussaka* and *gyros*, he loved all food equally. He was democratic that way.

"Yes. You really understand me now." She beamed.

After dinner with Sujaya, Sanjay drove to Mayank house. It had been quite an eventful day between Aditi and Sujaya. It was almost eleven when he rang their doorbell. A bleary-eyed Jayshree opened the door for him.

"Sorry. I didn't realize it was so late. Is Mayank sleeping?"

"No. Come in. We're both working on the Bay Networks project. You're right in time to cheer us up with your romantic escapades. I'll get Mayank for you. Do you want some coffee? I think I've had twenty cups till now."

The thought of food made his stomach rumble badly. He remembered the lovely lunch he had had yesterday. "By any chance, do you have any stuff left over from yesterday? I'm still hungry."

"How come? Didn't you have a date with Sujaya at the *Westin?*"

"You know about Sujaya?" he asked surprised.

Of course! In Hyderabad everybody knows everybody else. And everybody knows what you're doing. Get used to it. So didn't you have any dinner?"

"Barely. She's some virtuous, yoga freak. I think I could like her if I put my mind to it. I mean she really beautiful and she's a nice person. I don't know. Is this how it's supposed to be? How did you decide that you wanted to marry Mayank?"

"I don't know. I didn't decide. I just did it." Jayshree laughed and left to reheat the leftovers. When she came back with a plate of food Mayank had joined them.

"So what's up?" said Mayank as he came out and sat next to Sanjay. He was wearing rumpled pajamas and looked like he hadn't shaved. For the past four weeks, Jayshree and he were usually up till 3:00 working on the Bay Networks project. Bay Networks was Mayank's biggest and most demanding client. Without it he knew that it would be hard to sustain their company, Phoenix Soft. They were due to get a large project from BNI that would significantly increase the value of their company, but a lot depended on the performance of their current project.

"What's up with you?" asked Sanjay surprised, taking a bite of food. "You look like hell."

"Yeah. It's this stupid project. I think it's going to kill me. We don't have enough people working on it and it's really hard to train people on short notice. You don't want to apply for a job with us by any chance?"

"No. I don't want to get caught up in work until I get married. I'll get so engrossed in work that I won't have anytime for anything else. Getting married is my highest priority right now. Tell me, why did you marry Jayshree?"

Mayank looked at him blankly. "Uh...Umm. Let's see. She's nice."

"Thanks. That really helps," said Sanjay sarcastically. He thought about the matrimonial site that had been advertised on the television. He really should register on it.

"Hmm," said Mayank and they both sighed. Both were lost in their own problems.

BABY BLUES

Jayshree was in a terrible mood. She had been up late last night with Sanjay and Mayank and then the maid hadn't turned up that morning. Finally, the geyser had stopped working, forcing her to shower with cold water. She was now late for her meeting. An exasperated Mayank had left for the office without her, leaving her to deal with all the housework at home. She had finally driven herself to work. The Mayank she knew back in the US would never have left her alone to deal with a domestic crisis. India was definitely bringing out the male chauvinist in him.

She was still fuming when she walked into Mayank office. Mayank was groping Anju's stomach.

"Still can't feel anything," he said, concentrating hard and not noticing that Jayshree was standing near the door.

"Hmm...Maybe you should try a little lower," said Anju smiling.

"Yes. Yes. I think I can feel it now. My God. That's incredible!" he exclaimed, as he looked up at Anju.

"Hi," said Jayshree a little loudly. Both startled and turned guiltily towards her. Mayank's hand dropped to his side. He then realized that he hadn't really done anything to feel guilty about. Watching Anju get excited about the baby's movement had made him excited too. He had a sudden yearning to feel his baby moving inside Jayshree. He was tired of waiting for Jayshree to be ready. He wanted his own baby.

"Anju asked me if I wanted to feel her baby. I think it just kicked my hand. Isn't it incredible?" he asked, still feeling a bit stunned.

"That's just great. Anju if you don't mind, could I speak to Mayank? We have a meeting in five minutes." She knew that Anju and Mayank had done nothing wrong, but the sight of Mayank happily rubbing some other woman stomach felt weird. This was her Mayank. If he was going to rub anybody's tummy it should be hers. She felt a stabbing possessiveness in her heart that she hadn't felt in a long time. Why would she? He had never ever given her any reason to be jealous. She knew that he wanted to start a family. He had told her so many times, but somehow it had never seemed like the right time.

"What's wrong?" asked Mayank after Anju left his office, noting Jayshree's dark face. "Are you angry about Anju? It's no big deal. She just asked me if I wanted to feel the baby kick."

"Nothing's wrong. If you wanted to feel Anju's baby, well, there's nothing wrong with that," she told him coldly. "Should we start?" They discussed office matters for a while when Jayshree said, "Arvind has become very irregular. He comes in late and leaves early. He is always behind schedule and has caused a lot of problems during the last three months. Maybe we should fire him."

"Arvind has been with us from the beginning. He does good work. His mother is suffering from cancer so he has to take her to the doctor for her treatments. He has already spoken to me about it. Things work a bit differently here in India. We can't just fire people when we are already short-staffed," he said absentmindedly. "Why don't we have a baby too? We've been married for six years. How long do you want to wait?" It seemed like wherever he went, people around him were either in the process of having a baby or had just had a baby.

"I thought we would have a baby when we were settled. What's the rush? Anyway, this is hardly the time to be discussing this," she said embarrassed. The door to Mayank's office was open and she knew a couple of colleagues were keenly listening to their conversation while pretending to work.

"When is a good time to discuss this? We work all the time so why can't we discuss this now? All my relatives keep asking me about when we're going to have a baby. They think we have some problem," he said scandalized. "You know Anu *mami* gave me the address to some infertility clinic a few days ago and Ruby *chachi* wanted to know if you are cooperating with me." Even Amit, his cousin, had discreetly asked him if he was managing to get it up, in his typical Punjabi way. He had even offered to get him some special pills. That had really got him. He was too embarrassed to even mention it to Jayshree. She would have a good laugh.

"Cooperating?" she asked incensed. "You should have told her to mind her own business. Your relatives are not going to decide when we're going to have a baby. Anyway it's because of your relatives that we're not settled. There's always some wedding, or some family calamity or work crisis. And you don't help me with anything," she said hurt.

"It's not just my relatives. I want to have a baby. And what do you mean I don't help you with anything? This is India.

If you need help, hire somebody. Why do you need me?" he asked.

"But it used to be fun when we used to do things together," she whined.

"You think washing dishes and cleaning is fun? Then you do it because it's not fun for me." He sighed. "Look, when we're in India all this stuff will always be there. We have to make time if we want to have a family. If we keep waiting for the right time, it's never going to come and finally we'll be too old."

Jayshree was quiet. She knew that this day would come when Mayank would insist on starting a family. She did want to have kids but she didn't know why she kept postponing the inevitable and she didn't know how to explain how she felt to him. "You've changed since coming to India. You used to help me out so much in the US. Now you're always busy with your relatives leaving me to deal with everything in the house. Even this morning, you went off without me."

"But we were getting late for the meeting and you insisted on washing all the dishes before leaving. What was I supposed to do? Why couldn't you just leave them for tomorrow?" he argued.

"And then come home to a mountain of dirty dishes? That would be very nice."

"We could go out for dinner. What's the big deal? It's only the two of us. This is exactly the reason that I didn't get into my dad's business and move in with my parents. I wanted you to have some privacy. What else do you want me to do? If we had a baby, we could keep a full-time maid. We can have a good life here too, Shree. You just need to change the way you think a bit," he cajoled.

"Maybe after a couple of months, we could...." began Jayshree.

"I want to do it right now, Shree." Mayank said quietly. By now, Rahul and Sumit, their two colleagues in the adjacent cubicle, had completely stopped pretending that they were working and were leaning over their desks to listen to their conversation.

"What do you mean you want to do it right now? You're talking as if we should drop everything right this moment and start right now," she said sulkily.

When Mayank realized what he had said, he smiled sheepishly. "That won't be such a bad idea. Seriously Shree, do you know how long it's been? Two months. I've been counting. We're never going to have a baby like this. Why does this happen?" he asked morosely even though he knew why. Shree never initiated sex. He had deliberated stayed away from her to see if she would. She hadn't. It had hurt.

"I don't know. There's always something to be done. Or we're not together..." She looked at him helplessly.

"We have to make it a priority. In fact, we should go home right now," he said, feeling inspired.

Jayshree swallowed. She was actually getting a bit turned on and she knew by the look in Mayank's eyes that he was too. It was no big surprise considering how long it had been since they had done it. "You want to leave work at 11:00 and go home now?" she said uncertainly.

"Yes, why not?" he asked.

"I think you've lost your mind. But ok. Um...fine. If you can be spontaneous, I can be spontaneous. Let me get my purse." They both stepped out of his room. Sumit and Rahul were leaning over their cubicles with big grins on their faces.

"What? Get back to work." Mayank told both of them.

An hour later, both were lying lazily in their bed. Jayshree head was resting on Mayank's bare shoulder. Mayank was twirling her hair around his finger. He loved her long, silky hair. Especially when it was loose and spread all over him. A wave of affection washed over him. "We should do this more often," he said kissing the top of her head.

"Have sex or skip work?" she asked snuggling closer to Mayank under the covers. He looked so nice with his hair all mussed up.

"Both." He tugged gently at her hair so that he could look at her face. "So are we officially trying for a baby now?" he asked searching her face.

"I don't know. Whatever," she mumbled burying her face into his chest again. "I'm scared."

"Why? I promise I'll be there if you need me," he said turning her on her back and leaning over her. He placed his hand possessively over her stomach.

"We should be heading back to the office," she murmured reluctantly but made no move to get up. They had a lot of work to get done and they were also expected for dinner at Mayank's parent's house that evening.

"Are you kidding? There's no way I'm going back to the office and facing those guys again today. Is there anything to eat? It's almost lunchtime and I'm hungry," he said getting up. Jayshree stuck her tongue out at him. He was back to being a typical husband. She got up to get Mayank something to eat and thought about what she was going to wear for the dinner tonight. She hoped her mother-in-law hadn't gone overboard like she usually did.

MARGARITAS AND MATCH-MAKING

Dolly Arora bustled about her house getting things ready for her dinner party. She wanted it to be perfect because tonight was special. Mayank's friend, Sanjay, was coming to dinner. Mayank had told her that he was rich and single which naturally led her to her second best hobby which was match-making. She thought that he would make a perfect match for Swati, her sister's daughter. So she had also invited her sister's family for the dinner.

Pradeep Arora walked into the house just as Dolly was putting the final touches to the elaborate Mexican dinner that she had planned. Most of the meal had been ordered from *Cantina*, a restaurant famous for its delicious Mexican food, but Dolly always liked to add a few touches of her own to make any meal look like it was homemade. Today, she had whipped up a batch of *guacamole* to go with the *nachos*, *tacos*, *burritos* and *enchiladas* that she had ordered. She looked up at her husband and said, "Why don't you take out the tequila and whip up a batch of *margaritas*? It'll go with the Mexican dinner I planned?"

"*Arre*! Why do you always make this Mexican and Italian?

Why can't we just have regular *dal, chawal* and *subji* like other normal people?" Mayank's father was a typical Punjabi who liked his *paneer butter masala* and *dal makhani*. Although he had a sharp brain and had made a lot of money in his many businesses, he was set in his ways and didn't want to change his lifestyle. He was from a middle class family and started off selling scrap when he was twenty five years old. Within two years, he bought two taxis and started a taxi service. Now, he owned a major transport company and many petrol stations. While he was busy establishing his empire, his wife had been busy climbing up the social ladder. He grudgingly acknowledged that sometimes her contacts had helped him tremendously in his business. This was the only reason he tolerated her parties. If only she would serve some real food.

"He is a multimillionaire from America, Pradeep. We have to serve him food that he is familiar with. I think he be a good match for Swati, don't you think?"

He thought about Dolly's niece. She was worldly-wise twenty five-year-old fashion designer who changed boyfriends faster than she changed her clothes. Swati was on the lookout for a rich, well-connected husband who was willing to sponsor her fashion designing career without too much effort on her part. He wouldn't want a girl like that anywhere near his sons, so he presumed he wouldn't want her anywhere near his son's friend either.

"*Accha hi hoga.* I'm sure they'll be good for each other," he said diplomatically. "This Sanjay, he was born and brought up in Hyderabad, no? Indian *khana kyo nahi kahega?*" he asked, without expecting an answer and left before she could ask him any more uncomfortable questions.

An hour later, Mayank, his younger brother Jayant,

Jayshree, Sanjay, Swati, Swati's parents and her fifteen-year old brother Akhil were all seated in Dolly's luxurious living room enjoying the food that Dolly had laid out in the dining area. The older crowd, consisting of Pradeep and Swati's parents, were seated on the dining table discussing business, while Jayshree, Swati, Mayank and Sanjay were having their dinner in the living room. Swati had made it a point to sit next to Sanjay and her over-powering perfume was beginning to give him a mild headache.

"So you're in software," she purred crossing her legs and revealing more of her shapely leg. She moved closer to Sanjay. Her brother, who was alternately chewing on a large *burrito* while furiously punching the buttons of his Nintendo DS, looked up. "How will Uncle eat when you're practically sitting on his lap?" he muttered before going back to punching on his Nintendo furiously.

Swati glared at her brother. Sanjay almost choked on his *taco*, both by Akhil's comment and the fact that an over-grown hulk who badly needed a shave had just called him 'Uncle'. He then sadly acknowledged that he was probably old enough to be Akhil's uncle. "Yes," said Sanjay shifting an inch away from her. He was beginning to understand the purpose of this dinner. He turned to Mayank. "You could have warned me," he said accusingly.

"I did warn you. Swati's my mother's sister's daughter," said Mayank as if it explained everything.

"I'm a fashion designer," she said, trying again. "You're just come down from the US? Dolly Aunty says you're all alone here," she said sympathetically.

"Not really alone. I've plenty of friends and relatives here," he said politely. He really wasn't in the mood to chat with Swati and be scrutinized by her parents about whether he was good husband material or not. Sometimes, meeting girls felt like he was attending a job interview. Trying to get them to open up or shut up, fielding uncomfortable questions and putting his best foot forward was becoming a bit of a chore.

Just last evening, he had visited some acquaintances of his aunt who had a daughter to be married off. That meeting had been diametrically opposite of this one. The girl had been from a middle-class family and had been decked out in her best *Kancheevaram* sari and what looked like two kilos of solid gold jewellery. She had coyly brought out an array of snacks which included assorted *murukulus, masala vadas* and *bondas* which had reminded him of his childhood. He had felt a bit guilty of indulging himself with the food while the girl sat with a fixed smile on her face, her eyes darting appraisingly over him from time to time, while her father had quizzed him about his job and future plans.

"So are you planning on settling down here or are you going back to America?" asked Swati's mother bringing him back to the present.

"Right now, the plan is to settle down in Hyderabad," said Sanjay wondering if he should have brought along his bio-data or prepared some notes on Frequently Asked Questions. His aunt had actually asked him to prepare a bio-data that she could pass on to all her acquaintances. He had drawn the line at that. It had felt too desperate.

"Mayank said that you were offered a good post in SAP when they bought your company. Why didn't you take it? Why do you want to settle in India? Everybody else wants to go to America," asked Swati's father.

"I wanted to take a break to get married before I started

working again so I thought India was a good place to do that. There are a lot of opportunities here now," said Sanjay.

"After marriage, are you going to start your own company or apply for jobs?" asked Swati's father persistently.

Sanjay smiled even though his lips felt like they were glued together. "I haven't decided yet," he replied wondering how that affected his ability to be a good husband.

"Which car do you drive?" asked Akhil tearing himself away from his Nintendo for two minutes to add his own two cents.

"A BMW," said Sanjay putting his plate down. He had lost his appetite and felt a bit depressed. His love life did not look rosy.

"Which one? Dad has the 3 series," said Jayant, Mayank's younger brother, who had a tremendous respect for all motor vehicles, which is why he had joined his father in the transport business.

"740li."

"Wow. Is it an automatic or a stick shift?" asked Akhil, his eyes popping.

"Automatic."

"Can I take it for a ride?" begged Jayant.

"Sure," said Sanjay, fishing out his car keys from his pocket.

"No, you can't," said Mayank simultaneously. "He drives like a maniac. I don't think you should let him drive your car. He's already banged my car twice. I don't let him touch my car now," he said to Sanjay.

"But you let Jayshree drive your car even after she damaged it badly," protested Dolly. "Let the poor boy go have some fun."

"She was learning to drive a stick shift. It's not the same thing at all," said Mayank tersely, quickly glancing at Jayshree. Jayshree had been on the receiving end of his mother's comments all evening. She was now sitting with a stony face fiddling with her half-eaten *burrito*.

"Eat *Beti*. You haven't touched your food. I told Dolly to get some Indian food but she didn't listen. Nobody is touching this Mexican rubbish," said Mayank's father to Jayshree trying to cheer her up.

"I love Mexican food," said Swati in a feeble attempt to get everybody's attention back to her. "Don't you like Mexican food? You haven't finished your *burrito*. Shall I get you something else," she asked Sanjay.

"No thanks. I should leave. It's getting late."

"Oh. You can't leave now. You have to have some apple pie. Swati made it herself," exclaimed Dolly. "She's such a fabulous cook. She can cook all kinds of cuisines, Chinese, Continental, Indian, Italian," said Swati's mother.

"Maybe just a little bit," said Sanjay with a smile. He took out his phone to check if Ms Loveleen had replied to his comment. She had.

"Ah! The Credit Card Guy. I always look forward to your comments. They make me think a little bit more than I usually like to. I thought about your dilemma. The thing is you never really know how the future will pan out. Even the most ardent *Bharatiya Nari* might turn into a shrew five years down the line and make you miserable. What will you do then? Get a divorce? It's always wiser to entrust your heart and life to someone with whom you share a great friendship or chemistry with, instead of someone who just has great qualities that you like. Hope this helps," she had replied. Sanjay was thoughtful.

Swati left to serve the apple pie while Jayshree started collecting the used plates and putting them in the sink. Mayank went into the kitchen as Jayshree was putting away leftovers into the refrigerator. He put his arm around Jayshree's waist.

"I'm sorry," he said pulling her close to him.

"About what? You haven't done anything," said Jayshree moving away from him and wiping the kitchen counter. Before he could reply his mother appeared along with Swati's mother. They were discussing Sanjay.

"He seems like a nice boy," Swati's mother was saying excitedly. "I think Swati likes him too. He's rich and educated and so polite."

"Why don't you talk to him and find out what he thinks about Swati? *Kuch bath vath kar lo*," Dolly told Mayank.

"*Kya bath karu?* If he likes her, he'll tell me himself, Ma," Mayank replied. "You didn't want a South Indian daughter-in-law, so how come it's okay to have a South Indian son-in-law?" he asked sarcastically.

"He is rich with no parents. There are very few boys like that. *Apni* Swati will be like a queen in his house. Anyway, he's from America. He doesn't behave like a typical Telugu boy," she said dismissing his remarks.

"Whatever. Shree and I have to leave now. We have to go to work early tomorrow."

"Pah! Work! Work! All the time work! You people never have time to do anything. What is the use of having all this big business when your children are never around and have no intention of having any children either? All your father's property is a big waste," said Dolly to her son with disgust.

"That's not true. I'm always there whenever you need me.

Jayant *bhi* Papa *ko* business *mein* help *kar raha hai*. What more do you want? And for your information, Shree and I have decided that we are going to start trying for a baby from now on," Mayank retorted impulsively. The moment the words were out of his mouth, he wished he could take them back. It had been too soon to make such a dramatic announcement. His mother and aunt both hugged him tightly with delight.

"Oh *beta*! That's just great news," said his mother, hugging Jayshree who was looking at him with a murderous look on her face. Mayank's mother and aunt rushed into the living room to give the good news to Mayank's father and uncle.

"What the hell is wrong with you?" burst out Jayshree as soon as the two women left the kitchen. Mayank looked at her remorsefully before following his mother into the living room. His father and uncle patted him affectionately on his back. Swati hugged her cousin and announced, "Oh. I want to throw Jayshree a baby shower like they do in America. I wonder if Rekha will be available to plan the event."

"But she's not really pregnant yet," Mayank said feebly.

"I guess I should congratulate you both for your intentions," said Sanjay amused. He put his arm around Mayank's shoulder. "Is it customary to make an announcement in advance in your family?"

"No," replied Mayank mortified. "I don't know what it is? Whenever Shree and my mom are in the same room together, I can't do anything right."

"Are you in trouble with Jayshree?" Sanjay asked Mayank.

"I am always in trouble. Sometimes I just randomly tell her that I'm sorry and Shree tells me what it is that I'm sorry about," said Mayank wondering how to make a quick exit.

"You should enjoy your freedom as much as you can instead of trying to get married."

Later that night, Mayank and Jayshree got ready for bed. Jayshree hadn't spoken to him since they returned. She lay down on the bed and switched on her laptop and started checking her e-mails.

"I didn't mean to tell the whole world," he said stroking the crook of her arm. "The words just slipped out of my mouth."

"Go to sleep," said Jayshree flicking his hand away.

He took the laptop away from her and held her hand caressing the inside of her palm. "You do realize that now that I've told the whole world we'll have to try extra hard to make it happen fast."

She withdrew her hand, fluffed up her pillows and turned away from him to go to sleep. "You're an idiot," she mumbled into the pillow.

"We can't waste a single night now. We might have to do it twice or thrice a day," he said seriously.

Jayshree smothered a smile but did not give in. She buried herself in her pillow and went off to sleep.

Mayank sighed. "Nobody's happy with me," he said sadly.

CONFESSING OVER COFFEE

After his disastrous date with Sujaya, Sanjay realized he could no longer rely on friends and relatives to fix him up with a suitable bride. He needed to take matters into his own hands. He googled *Desi Matrimony*, the website that promised to find the perfect match at the perfect price. Who said money can't buy love, he thought grandly as he waited for the page to load. The site tantalizingly revealed bits and pieces of itself with the speed of a stripper who charged by the hour. He cursed his service provider and then cursed himself for not trying the internet before. After spending so many years being part of the mobile banking revolution, he had relied on Attamma and Aditi to find him a wife. An aging aunt and a...a...who was Aditi anyway? She wasn't even a friend. She was just some nutcase who did whatever she pleased whenever the mood struck her.

He shouldn't think about Aditi, he chided himself sternly. She was a total flake and a bit too easy-going for his comfort. He didn't want to marry someone like that. Imagine ditching a guy who was in love with you and wanted to marry you. It's not like he was looking to marry a virgin but Aditi took casual relationships to the next level. Anyway, she was one of those feminist types who thought getting married was similar to dying, so there was no point in constantly thinking about her. He could just imagine what Attamma would think about someone like Aditi.

As he browsed the website, he could hear Attamma, his father's sister, banging pots and pans in the kitchen. She and Mamaiya were spending the weekend with him. They had a son, Ajay, who had settled down in the US, so they came and stayed with him whenever they got bored. Sometimes he invited them over when he needed a little TLC. Attamma had made vague noises about meeting her cousin's husband's friend's daughter at a wedding who she claimed was perfect for him. The only problem with the alliance, according to her, was the girl's age. The girl was nineteen.

Mamaiya had strenuously denied that the age gap was a problem. "In olden days," he had said sagely, "wives were ten to fifteen years younger than their husbands so that they were young enough to care for them in their old age." That was the first time Sanjay had heard of this. He thought children were supposed to take care of their parents in their old age. In any case, there was no way he could even think of marrying somebody who was nineteen years old. The word 'paedophile' kept flashing before his eyes in bright blue neon whenever he did. He didn't say that to Mamaiya though. Attamma was almost fourteen years younger to him.

When the site finally loaded, he registered himself as a member of the site. Things went smoothly till he was asked about his sub-caste. Kandavara? Dhima? Kayastha? Niyogi? Who were all these people? He hadn't realized there were so many different types of Brahmins. He was tempted to ask his aunt but was terrified of the torrential rambling about his grandfather and great grandfather that might follow such a question. He ignored the question.

When he finally clicked the submit button, the website opened a whole treasure chest of beautiful, intelligent, nubile, young women for his selection. Well, not all of them were beautiful. Or young. Or particularly intelligent.

He read one profile. "Hello To readers of this. My Name is Anuradha. I am single. I dont have a boy, If any one want to marry to me please to ask my mother or father or sister or brother or write to me. I am not a good college but I working all day in the field in bangaluru. Thanks and Regards. PS i want very simple boy from brahmin educated family. I have large knowledge of all homework," it said.

Homework? She meant housework, he guessed. What did she mean…she works in the field in Bangalore? Maybe she was in Marketing. And maybe he shouldn't have given out his real name or phone number or address.

He read another profile. "Hello dear friends. I enjoys every moments of life. I am born to friend and like people. Because friendship is a first step of love. I am looking for my heart in one who will love me so much. Because I love myself a lot. If u think you can love me ten times than me then call me. We can live in each other's heart!!!" it claimed enthusiastically.

Sanjay's heart slowed down and sank. Seriously? What the hell, he thought. Perfect match for the perfect price, indeed. He looked up another website, *JhatpatShaadi.com,* which called itself a premium website for the elite. It charged American citizens $500 for a four-month membership. Money could buy you love but it didn't come cheap, he thought amazed.

Once he was registered, he was asked to fill up a questionnaire of his requirements. When he was done, the system spewed out the photos of all the girls that matched his prerequisites. He glanced through the photos feeling lost. Everybody looked good on paper. How was he supposed to figure out the right one for him? He clicked on the profile of a girl called Uma Reddy. She was an accountant at Ernst and Young and listed her hobbies as cooking and trying out different cuisines. It could work, he thought. They had stuff in common. He sent her a message. A pop-up window informed him that a message had been sent to Uma and that he should wait for her reply. God only knew when that would materialize, he thought resigned. He should have used carrier pigeons or a message in a bottle. That would probably show results faster.

He explored some of the other sites but was disappointed. Ultimately, it all came down to the same thing, he realized. You meet a total stranger in an awkward setting and decide if you want to spend the rest of your life with her. Why didn't somebody come up with a system that would help people find a partner in a more pleasant manner, he mused, scratching his chin.

"*Enti*, Sanjay? Are you going to sit on the computer all day? Come and talk to us before we leave," said Attamma crossly. Sanjay shut down his laptop guiltily and went and sat with his aunt and uncle.

"So should I talk to the girls parents?" asked his aunt hopefully. "You can go see her this weekend." She was getting tired of searching for girls for Sanjay. It had been so easy to find a bride for Ajay. He was not so fussy and so old. And he earned in dollars. Everybody said that Sanjay was a smart boy but how smart could he be if he left a perfectly good job in America to come and sit idle in Hyderabad. All he did all day was sit on his computer, go to the gym or wander around aimlessly all around

Hyderabad. He didn't even bother to eat his meals in time. She took in his unshaven face and rumpled clothes. She cursed her brother for dying early without fulfilling all his responsibilities.

"No, Attamma. She's too young," protested Sanjay.

"So where will we find a woman your age for you? They are all married, no? Bah! *Adi entamatram upayogam ledu*...it's no use," said his aunt unhappily.

"It's okay. I rather be unmarried than be married to the wrong person," said Sanjay amused.

"Good. You will die alone. Like your father," she said angrily. Sanjay was silent. She started to cry. "I'm sorry. You poor boy."

"I'm fine," he said nonchalantly. He was used to his aunt's dramatics.

"We should go now," said his uncle awkwardly.

"I'll drop you. It's on my way," said Sanjay, getting up with them.

"How is Koti on your way?" asked his aunt suspiciously. "We'll take an auto."

"No. I'll drop you," he replied firmly.

After dropping his uncle and aunt, Sanjay stopped at *Crossword* to buy some books. A section of the store had been cordoned off for an event. He went closer to investigate. He found Aditi sitting in the middle of the gathering doing a book reading. He watched as she read from her book, spectacles perched seriously at the tip of her nose. Surprisingly, there were no men in the audience. Ladies were dabbing at their eyes discreetly. His curiosity was piqued. He went up to the gathering and took a seat in the corner. The only thing he could figure out about the story was that there was a French man who was in love with a deaf Indian girl who refused to marry him because she didn't want to leave her Alzheimer's-stricken mother alone. He quickly understood why there weren't any men around.

Aditi looked up when she was done and saw Sanjay sitting in the audience. She waved at him enthusiastically taking off her spectacles. She signed some books and hugged some women. Some women wanted to discuss some points about the book and others took photos with her. When the crowd thinned out, she came and sat next to him. "What are you doing here?" she asked surprised.

"I was buying some books," he explained.

"Mine?" she asked hopefully.

"No. Well, okay maybe," he agreed. "Is it a new book?"

Aditi sighed. "I wish. I haven't had a book out now for almost two years. I'm suffering from the most horrendous writer's block. I haven't written anything worthwhile for a year now…just a blog, some articles and short stories here and there. Why do think I'm wasting my time with parties, book readings and ribbon cuttings. If I had something worthwhile to write about, I'd be at home writing. You know, sometimes I get up in the middle of the night and wonder if I'm ever going to do anything great in my life ever again."

Sanjay stared at her. It was exactly the way he felt sometimes. "Do you want to have coffee or something? There's a coffee shop in the store." He took her by the arm and almost dragged her to the in-house coffee shop. "Tell me about your writer's block," he demanded.

"What's wrong with you?" she grumbled rubbing her arm. "Why do want to know about my writer's block?"

He ordered two cappuccinos and sat back in his chair. "Because I'm have the same problem."

"You're not a writer," she said confused, taking off her spectacles.

"Not about writing," he corrected. "About never doing anything great in my life ever again." He picked up her glasses and examined them. "This is plain glass."

"It makes me look more intellectual," she explained. "At least you made a lot of money. 'Critically-acclaimed' doesn't always translate to bushels of cash, you know. I have to stoop to attending store openings and giving talks to make some decent money. It's really humiliating sometimes. My parents think I should go back to my copy-writer's job or get married. I have a pretty high-end lifestyle to support and writing is not exactly a secure job."

Sanjay laughed at her honesty and put her glasses back on her nose. It just made her look cuter. He looked away at a distance. "Sometimes I feel like I'm on this roller-coaster and I've passed the high-point of my life and things will only go downhill from here," he confided softly. Aditi was looking at him intently. It was so great to meet somebody who was in the same situation as him. Most people only envied him and told him to go on a world cruise. He debated about whether he should tell her about the grand idea he had this afternoon while browsing matrimonial sites. Aditi was the only person crazy enough to understand. "I'm thinking of starting a dating website," he confessed.

She looked at him skeptically. "From getting married to starting a dating website. Aren't you getting a little obsessed with marriage? I thought you were doing something high-tech in finance before. A dating website doesn't sound like you."

"My website is high-tech. Online dating is the second highest money generator on the net. Imagine a place where you could state your requirements and the system sent you an SMS whenever another member who met your prerequisites was within fifty feet of you. You can then download their photo and bio and decide if you want to meet them or not. If you don't like them, you ignore them without spending a whole agonizing evening getting to know them. If you like what you see, you can meet them and take things forward. Sort of an arranged cum love marriage," he told her.

Aditi shook her head. "How can you decide whether you like somebody or not with one look? Spending time with a person helps you figure out if you're compatible or not. People nowadays don't want to make any effort. Instant dating. Instant communication. Instant sex," she said sadly. "Whatever happened to romance?"

"You can figure out a lot about a person in one look. It's a scientifically proven fact that a person takes three minutes to decide if they want to go out with somebody or not. Look at that guy over there. Do you want to get to know him?" he pointed at a short, bespectacled man wearing a yellow T-shirt, baggy grey trousers and tennis shoes.

Aditi turned to look and her eyes widened. "Of course," she lied.

"Fine. Ask him out," he challenged, his eyes twinkling.

Aditi swallowed. "I think it's rude to sit with one guy and ask another guy out," she said virtuously.

"He's probably really romantic. How will you know unless you go out with him?" he asked silkily. "Shall I tell him you want to get to know him better?"

"Yes," she replied bravely but he could see the panic in her eyes. Sanjay stood up. "Wait," she choked out. "I can't do it. I can't."

"See? It proves my point," he said with satisfaction. But deep inside, he was far from satisfied. It might take three minutes to get attracted to Aditi but something told him it would take a lifetime to try to figure her out. Stop thinking of Aditi, he admonished himself. Aditi didn't want to get married. If he kept repeating that to himself over and over, it might register in his brain sometime soon.

MIXED MESSAGES

Sanjay looked up from his laptop and glanced at the clock. It was almost five o'clock in the evening. He had been so engrossed in developing the prototype of his dating application that he had skipped lunch. He sighed. He needed a wife to take care of these little details. Aditi's disapproving face flashed in his mind. It was a good thing Aditi couldn't read his mind right now. She would have given him an hour-long lecture about respecting women and not equating them with cooking and cleaning.

He went into the kitchen to make himself some tea and toast. Atleast he didn't have to worry about what to have for dinner. Mayank was celebrating his birthday at *Rain* tonight. Thinking of the party made him think of Uma. He debated about whether he should take Uma to Mayank's party at *Rain*.

Uma had finally replied to his email and they had gone out a couple of times but there had not been much chemistry between them even thought she had a good grasp of finance and was interesting to talk to. He brushed off his misgivings. Attraction would develop when they got to know each other better. This was how it was when people had an arranged marriage. You could both be reading the same book, but still not be on the same page. Eventually they would catch up with each other. He shouldn't be picky.

The thought of introducing Uma to the others seemed like a good idea. It was always nice to know if your wife got along with your friends. After all, Mayank, Jayshree and Aditi were definitely part of his life now. He didn't think he wanted to be with Uma if she didn't get along with them. He hoped that Uma wouldn't think that he was getting serious about her by introducing her to his friends. He leaned back in his chair and smiled. He was so full of good ideas today.

He logged onto Ms Loveleen's Blog to check out her latest article titled 'Good-time Girls Vs Take-home Girls'. Ms Loveleen had become his love guru and he was addicted to her. "The fact of the matter is, at the end of the day, there are no good-time girls or take-home girls. When you're madly in love with someone, she's the one you want to take home," concluded the article.

Sanjay frowned. Was Aditi a good-time girl? He definitely wanted to take her home and have a good time with her for as long as possible. He wondered briefly about what he was doing with Uma when he was always having insane thoughts about Aditi, but pushed them aside. Nothing that he had done lately made a lot of sense.

Later that evening, the focus of his thoughts was sitting in *Rain* with Sharad blissfully unaware of just how much a certain person was thinking about her. She sipped her cosmopolitan slowly. She had met Sharad at the gym and immediately hit it off. Sharad owned a construction company. She hadn't bothered to find out which one. Who cared where he worked? She didn't even know what his last name was, for that matter. When she had watched him do two hundred crunches in his sweat-soaked tank top revealing his powerful biceps and shoulders, she knew she was hooked. When Mayank had invited her for his birthday party, she had asked him if she could bring Sharad along and he had agreed.

Sharad was fun-loving, uncomplicated and had a good sense of humour. He had just gone through a messy break-up and had made it perfectly clear that he was not looking for a girlfriend…just some female company when it got lonely. It was the ideal situation as far as she was concerned. It kept things light between them so she didn't have to lie to him all the time. It was quite a relief.

When she had told him that she was The Aditi Patil, author of *The Gumohar Tree* and *East Meets West*, he had immediately asked her to loan him the books so that he could read them.

"So, how did you like my books?" she asked him.

"Hmm…okay. Good job," he said taking a sip of his beer.

"Did you actually read the whole thing?" she asked amazed. She had yet to meet a guy who had read an entire novel written by her. Most found it too cranky. "Did you think that Kiran did the right thing by leaving?"

Sharad froze. "Of course." He took another sip of his beer and glanced at her nervously.

"Liar. You didn't read my books did you?" she said laughing.

"I prefer mysteries and thrillers. I think if you put a murder or two in your stories it could really spice things up a bit," he admitted ruefully.

"The only spicing up that happens in romance novels is the hero and heroine kissing. Dead bodies are not romantic, darling," she said kissing him on the cheek. She liked being with Sharad.

They were soon joined by Mayank, Jayshree, Sanjay and Uma. After the introductions were made, Aditi learnt that Sanjay had met Uma through one of the online matrimonials. She was dressed in formal trousers and a sensible top and it looked like she had come directly from work.

So he was still looking for his soulmate, thought Aditi amused. He hadn't called Sujaya back, so she had assumed he wasn't interested. The mousy, quiet girl sitting next to him didn't look like his soulmate either, but she didn't think it was the right time to point that out to him. She was suddenly doubly glad that she had come with Sharad. She leaned her head on Sharad's shoulder.

Sanjay watched Aditi cosy up to the Bradley Cooper look-alike. He had forgotten what his name was and he was reasonably sure Aditi had too. She was almost stuck to him when there was a good ten inches of empty space with which she could sit quite comfortably. He couldn't understand couples who engaged in public displays of affection. He always thought that there was a whiff of insecurity behind all that public mauling. He had never seen Mayank and Jayshree clinging on to each other like that and they were the most solid couple he had ever known. He was glad he had brought Uma along even though she looked pretty uncomfortable sitting with a group of strangers.

The waiter came along and took their orders. Mayank and Sanjay ordered whiskies, while Jayshree and Aditi ordered white wine. After much coaxing, Uma was talked into ordering a cola.

"A Pepsi, really?" asked Sanjay disappointed. He didn't have too much respect for people who drank soft drinks after the age of twenty-five. I need to get married...it doesn't matter what they eat or drink, he reminded himself. But deep down in his heart, he just couldn't understand people who didn't drink. It was good for the heart and drunken sex was the best sex. How could anybody refuse health and happiness in one gulp?

"So is this the first time you two are seeing each other?" Mayank asked Sanjay loudly. The music had been turned on high and it was getting difficult to speak to each other. Jayshree asked Mayank to dance but he gave her a grumpy look. He couldn't believe that she had bought him a boring sweatshirt for his birthday, when he'd been hinting about the Tag Heuer watch for the past one month. He had even casually e-mailed the ad to her.

"No. We met at your parent's anniversary and at your place for lunch, remember?" replied Sanjay frowning at Aditi. She was giggling and leaning close to Sharad to listen to what he was saying. Sharad had his hand on her thigh and was whispering in her ear.

Mayank looked at Sanjay and then looked at Aditi. "I was talking about Uma," he said wryly.

"Oh." Sanjay had the grace to look embarrassed. "No. We've been out twice before. She's a fantastic accountant. She's given me really good investment advice. I've saved a ton ever since I met her. She's pretty well-versed in US taxation laws as well. You should try her out."

"Just think about how much money you'll save if you married her," said Mayank with a twinkle in his eyes.

"Yeah. There's that," said Sanjay unenthusiastically.

Aditi grabbed Sharad's hand and led him to the dance floor. She looked disgustingly happy. Why don't they just get a room, Sanjay thought. Looking at them, Jayshree almost dragged Mayank to the dance floor. Mayank gave her a dirty look but finally relented. He still hadn't forgiven her for the baggy, grey sweatshirt though.

"I did get you your stupid watch. It's at home," she whispered in his ear, linking her arm with his.

"Oh? Why didn't you tell me before?" he asked brightening.

"I wanted it to be a surprise," she said and pulled him towards the dance floor leaving Sanjay alone with Uma.

Sanjay smiled awkwardly at Uma. She smiled back at him nervously. He hoped she didn't expect him to dance with her. Because Google would have to acquire Apple before that could happen. He could tell by the way she was clutching her Pepsi glass that dancing with him would be an equally painful experience for her as well. How was he supposed to marry her when he didn't even want to dance with her? He wondered briefly if she was a virgin. A thirty-year-old virgin? In India, anything was possible. He took out his phone and tried to look busy. How the hell did people have arranged marriages?

Aditi and Sharad returned sweaty and laughing. Aditi had a sip of her drink and said something animatedly into Sharad's ear. Sharad smiled. Sanjay could feel the pheromones buzzing between them. Mayank and Jayshree returned and collapsed on the sofa. Even they were holding hands. It looked like everybody was getting laid tonight except for him. He felt a bit lonely.

A *Bhangra* number came on. Mayank took Aditi's hand and lead her to the dance floor. "South Indian's don't know how to dance. Come."

"Six years of *Bharatnatyam* and Mayank doesn't consider that dancing," commented Jayshree sadly.

"Okay. But this is your birthday dance. Only once. I'm exhausted," said Aditi laughing.

Sanjay watched Aditi dance with Mayank. At one point Mayank yelled something in Aditi's ear and she threw her head back and laughed.

"Why don't you ask her to dance?" asked Jayshree quietly.

"I don't dance. Anyway, what's the point of one dance? I'm looking for something else," he said finishing his whisky.

When Mayank and Aditi were back, everybody handed Mayank his presents. Aditi gave him an autographed copy of her most recent book. Sanjay promised him he had an eighteen-year-old Highland Park in the car for him. Mayank held Aditi's book and flipped through it. "This is what I really wanted all my life, Aditi," he said sarcastically.

When the gift-giving was done, Mayank cut his birthday cake and Aditi ragged him about the three candles that were placed on the cake. "One for each decade, huh, Mayank?" she said naughtily.

After all the festivities, Sharad excused himself saying he had an early morning plane to catch. Sanjay felt inexplicably lighter. Mayank offered to drop Aditi home but Sanjay intervened. "Your house is on my way home. I can drop you back," he said lightly.

"Oh. I don't want to intrude on your date," she said embarrassed, looking at Uma.

"It's no problem. I can drop Uma and drop you home," he said quickly without noticing the quizzical looks that Uma was giving him.

After dropping Uma, Sanjay made his way towards Aditi's house. The main road near Aditi's house was jammed with cars and policemen were everywhere.

"Shit," said Sanjay when he realized what was happening. This had to happen tonight of all nights. "The cops are checking for drunken driving."

"How many drinks did you have?" said Aditi concerned.

"Maybe three. Maybe more. I wasn't counting," he replied unhappily.

Aditi looked around the car. She spied a jacket in the corner. She took it and began to stuff it under her blouse.

"What are you doing?" asked Sanjay, his eyes widening as Aditi smoothened the jacket under blouse.

"See that young policeman there? Tell him I'm in labour and that we have to go," she demanded.

Sanjay looked at her and then at the policeman. He opened his mouth and closed it again. He shook his head. "I can't," he said helplessly. "I can't do that."

"God, you're hopeless!" She called out to the policeman while Sanjay sweated nervously beside her. Aditi explained the situation to the man making a special effort to look sickly and harassed. Sanjay stared at the steering wheel, only looking up to smile weakly at the policeman when Aditi was done talking. At least he didn't need to pretend to be nervous. He was humongously nervous. The policeman spoke on his walkie-talkie and started moving the other cars out of their way. When he had cleared a path for them, he came up to them and poked his head through the window.

"Good luck, Madam. Sorry for the inconvenience," said the young inspector shyly.

"Thank you so much," said Aditi, giving him her most dazzling smile. Sanjay and the inspector both stared at her entranced. "Come on. We have to go to the hospital, remember?" she said to a dazed Sanjay, who nodded and started the car.

Sanjay took a u-turn and drove in the direction opposite to Aditi's house. He turned into the road that led to the highway. The miles flew quickly and soon they were at the outskirts of the city. Aditi watched in fascination as they went further and further away from her house. It finally got so deserted that Aditi could no longer hold in her curiosity. "Where are you taking me? Did anybody tell you, you're a little weird?"

He turned to her in surprise. "Sorry. I like driving in the dark. I didn't realize how it must look. I can go back if you like," he said looking at her anxiously. "I didn't think you'd mind, considering that you were pregnant and just delivered my jacket a few minutes ago. And you think I'm weird." He shook his head in amazement.

Aditi smiled. "It's okay. Why do you like dark places? Are you a vampire or something? You should have got Uma here, you know. Not me. You spent the whole evening ignoring her. It's no surprise you can't get a girl."

"Uma doesn't look like the type to take long drives. Besides, I would have got caught if I were with her," he smirked, turning into a small lane that led to a hill. Sanjay concentrated on the winding, curvy road until he reached the top of the hill. Finally, he frowned at her. "I only like quiet, dark places because it helps me think clearly. Why would that make me a vampire? Is that how you think of me?"

"Oh! It's a compliment. Vampires are pretty hot these days. Almost as hot as eccentric, tech millionaires. Which you already are, so can drop the dark, broody looks you've been giving me all evening," Aditi told him.

Sanjay was confused. Did she mean that he was hot? It would be the first time a girl as beautiful as Aditi had called him hot. Actually, it would be the first time any girl had called him hot. He was too embarrassed to ask her to clarify her statement. Dark and broody and hot? People always found him serious. He was Peter Parker. Maybe Bruce Wayne on a good day. When did he turn into Batman? Was Batman a vampire or just a man in weird clothes with a great car? It was hard to keep track nowadays. He sighed. Why did he end up thinking about ridiculous stuff whenever he was with Aditi?

He drove till the tiny lane ended into the most spectacular view of the city. He opened the car door and got out. Aditi followed. She could see the lights of the multinational office buildings twinkling at a distance between the magnificent rocks balancing precariously over each other.

"Uma likes my dark, brooding tech millionaire image. She thinks she can do a good job of managing my money," said Sanjay suddenly, turning towards her.

"That's always a good quality in a wife," said Aditi primly. Sanjay looked at her to see if she was serious. She looked back at him solemnly but soon gave him a slow grin. They both laughed.

He sat on the hood of the car and stretched out, leaning against the windshield with his hands behind his head. "Why didn't you leave with Sharad?" he asked after a little while. "What sort of guy leaves a girl like you alone in a pub?"

"Sharad is just a friend and I wasn't alone. I was with you guys, remember?" she protested, carefully climbing onto the hood of the car. "Are you sure it's okay to do this? I don't want to spoil your car."

"This car is designed to withstand a head-on collision. You're negligible weight is not going to damage it," said Sanjay amused. "How is the writing going?"

"Good. Not good. I'm not sure," she said suddenly serious. "I'm trying to sex up my writing a little bit. That's what my publisher wants me to do for my new book. It's what the new generation want. He thinks my novels are getting monotonous."

Sanjay wished he hadn't brought up the topic of her writing. He liked it when she was being crazy and zany and giggly. He wished she would be that way all the time. "I'm no writer, but I can understand the pressure of creating something. Do whatever feels right and what you believe in, not what people tell you do. At the end of the day, you have to be true to yourself."

"Is that what you're doing with your website? Being true to yourself?" Aditi turned her beautiful, hazel eyes on him appraisingly.

"If it's popular, it'll make money. That's always been my goal in life," said Sanjay shrugging.

"Right," said Aditi. And she should take the high road and be poor and unpopular, she fumed. Why did she feel a bit disappointed? So what if he was obsessed with money? It was none of her business.

CAN'T FIGHT CHEMISTRY

Sanjay was at home watching television. His life had finally settled into a comfortable routine. He had begun testing his application. The initial response had been good and he was feeling good about his work. He had also bought a house and was in the process of furnishing it. It was a four-bedroom townhouse in a decent housing complex. The living room had a high ceiling with beautiful French windows that led into a beautifully landscaped terrace garden. It was spacious but it wasn't so large that he felt overwhelmed by the space when he was alone.

His new neighbours were incredibly friendly and helpful too. There had been the lady in house number 23 who had weird, turmeric-stained feet but a heart of gold. She regularly sent him either some *lemon rice*, or *puliyogere* or *bisi bele bhaat*. Then, there was the French couple in house 16 who had invited him over for some wine and cheese and talked about the Eurozone crisis.

He had spent the past two weeks repeatedly calling the electrician to install his home theatre system but the guy was having an unbelievable amount of bad luck. He had suffered from typhoid, dengue and malaria...all in the span of one month. Then, his older son passed away. The final tragedy had been the death of his mother four days ago.

Sanjay had been so frustrated with his excuses that he had decided to mount his Bose speakers himself. He had been drilling a hole in the wall with his power drill when the drill bit broke and injured his hand. When he was in the US, he did this kind of work all the time but out there most houses were made of wood. He didn't realize that it was easier to drill through wood than brick and cement. He had managed to get himself to a doctor for some emergency first-aid, but his hand still hurt and oozed blood occasionally. Today was the second day and he had just about managed to put on trackpants and a loose, sleeveless T-shirt. He hadn't worked for the past two days and he was going crazy.

The doorbell rang. He wondered if it was the pizza he had ordered and went to open the door. Aditi stood outside. "Hi," she said stepping in without waiting for him to invite her in. "What have you been up to? Moved into a new house and didn't even inform anybody?" she reproached him while she casually strolled into his house. She was a wearing a silky, strapless blouse with jeans. She looked gorgeous as usual. Sanjay wondered how her blouse didn't just slither down her body. Only a woman with boobs that had the perfect combination of mass, volume and density like Aditi could perform this feat of anti-gravity, he realized. He got his mind off her boobs. What was he thinking? The pain-killers he had taken were obviously affecting his brain.

"Nice house. How come you haven't invited any of us home yet? No house-warming party?" she asked after a cursory glance.

"I didn't think you'd have the time. You been pretty busy," said Sanjay. Aditi and Sharad looked very happy the last time he had seen them together. He hadn't wanted to intrude.

"Oh. I'm not busy at all. I have all the time in the world," she said her eyes resting on his hand. "What happened to your hand? Does it hurt?" She searched for a place to sit but gave up. "How are you living in this place?" she said exasperated.

"I pretend I'm camping," he said impishly, pointing to the mattress that was lying in the corner of his office that was also temporarily his dining room and bedroom. The kitchen and the office were the only two rooms that were somewhat complete because the builder had promised him a fully-functional, custom-built kitchen at the time of delivery. The office was partly done because he couldn't survive without it. The rest of the house was driving him crazy and he was pretending that it didn't exist.

At the moment, all the other rooms were lying in various stages of completion because the carpenter turned out to be a distant relative of the electrician and had been afflicted with pretty much the same problems as the electrician. The only difference was that the carpenter had suffered from pneumonia. He had even shown Sanjay the medical bills to prove it. After extracting a loan of fifty thousand rupees from Sanjay to pay his hospital bills, he was merrily absconding leaving Sanjay in a house that looked like it was hit by a tornado.

Sanjay suddenly felt happier. His unfinished house and throbbing hand had begun to depress him a bit. It was amazing how Aditi always managed to cheer him up. The fact that she was alone, without a man trailing behind her like a lamb, was making him hugely estatic. Or maybe it was just the pain pills that were making him happy. He realized that he didn't care.

"Do you need any help with your hand or your house," she asked sympathetically. He was looking kind of lost today. She avoided looking at his hand. There was a tiny bit of blood that had seeped through the white dressing and it was making her queasy. She looked at his left bicep and shoulder. That wasn't a very good idea either. A thick vein emphasized his smooth, toned arm. The nerd had muscles, she thought amazed. He must work out. She shifted her gaze to the base of his neck. Tiny, bristly hair was poking out endearingly all over his jawline. Damn. That looked good too. She looked at his chest. Longer, silkier hair covered the smooth pectoral muscles and disappeared under his tank top. Her eyes drifted lower. The stomach looked toned too. Against her better judgement, her eyes fell lower. Oh my God, she thought, quickly bringing her eyes back to his face. Where was she supposed to look? She hoped he hadn't noticed the detour her eyes had taken.

He hadn't. He was too pre-occupied with his own thoughts. "The hand will be okay in a day or two. Any help with the house is always welcome," he was saying, smiling. He scratched his unshaven chin thoughtfully. "The house could do with a feminine touch." He didn't want to think about the other parts of him that were also craving a feminine touch. It had been so damn long since Sheetal. Aditi's touch would do nicely, he thought frustrated. Very, very nicely.

Aditi quickly went into his office to distract herself. Sanjay followed. He watched as she inspected his extensive vintage wine and Single Malt collection without comment. He resisted the urge to hide them. She probably thought he was a drunk now. His appearance right now would certainly match that observation. "Do you want something to drink?"

"Red wine will do for me, if you have it," she replied.

Sanjay went to kitchen and took out an opened bottle of a Californian red wine. He hoped Aditi would enjoy it. He poured it in two glasses. The doorbell rang again. It was the pizza he had ordered. Sanjay brought the pizza and wine into the office. Aditi was sitting cross-legged on his mattress. He turned to Aditi with a serious expression and gave her the wine. "So why are you here, Aditi?"

She helped herself to the pizza and looked up. "I wanted to see how you were doing. That's all," she said looking back at him steadily. He was twirling his wine glass and sniffing it thoughtfully like she had seen people do on television.

"I'm doing fine except that my house looks like a battlefield. Anything else you want to tell me?" He sat down cross-legged on the mattress in front of her, his knees touching hers.

There was something strangely intimate about the whole thing, thought Aditi. Boards of ply and wood were stacked in a corner. Half-opened cartons were lying around carelessly all over the place. The house was dusty and her clothes were dirty. And they were sipping wine and eating pizza in the middle of it all. It felt more romantic than sitting in a Michelin-star restaurant in Paris.

Sanjay sighed. "Can you be honest for a second and admit we are kind of attracted to each other?"

Aditi ignored him and sipped her wine. She should leave. This was exactly what she didn't want. Panic shot through her and she tried to get up. Sanjay stopped her.

"What? I just said something. Are you going to pretend I didn't say anything?" he asked, holding her arm tightly. She was forced to look into his eyes.

She swallowed the pizza she was chewing. "Well, maybe just a little bit."

"Maybe a little bit, what?" he said frustrated.

"Maybe I like you a little bit," she mumbled when he had almost given up.

He grinned. "So what are we going to do about it?"

"Nothing," she said shortly. "Nothing has really changed. You want to get married. I don't. There's no future there."

"We don't have to think about getting married immediately. We can see each other for a little while and see what happens," he said.

"So for how long will we be seeing each other before you start putting on the pressure to get married?" asked Aditi cautiously.

Sanjay smiled. "How about a week or two?"

Aditi snorted. "I was thinking more like never."

Sanjay stared at her with disbelief. "That's never going to happen. I want to have a family before I'm forty and now that I know that you like me too, I can't let you go."

"But how can it work?" she asked earnestly.

He stared into space and digested the question for a few moments. "What do you want in the future, Aditi? I mean twenty years from now, where do you see yourself? Mayank, Jayshree, Sujaya are all going to have kids and get busy with their lives. You're not going to be hanging around them all the time like you do now, you know. Doesn't that scare you? Because it scares the hell out of me."

"That's not going to happen to me. I'm a famous author. Okay, maybe I haven't written in a while, but I haven't given up yet," she said indignantly.

"I'm not telling you to give up. I'm just saying that maybe one day your books won't sell anymore or maybe you'll get bored of writing them. Or maybe one day you won't look so great in your tiny designer clothes. Don't you want somebody to be by your side then?"

"You think I look great?" she said cheering up.

"Out of everything I said that's the only thing you heard? You're so hopeless," he said exasperated as he leaned back and looked away.

Aditi caught his hand. "I heard everything else. I was just thinking it's the first compliment you've ever given me. You're mostly telling me I'm crazy or I'm wrong."

He grinned and his eyes crinkled at the corners. Her heart skipped a beat. "I'm sorry. You're a very, very beautiful and sweet girl, but you already know that."

"So what do you want to do, Sanjay? Get married? Then five years down the line we'll be yelling at each other and throwing things at each other. Oh my God. Kill me now," she said as she stabbed herself with an imaginary knife.

Sanjay laughed. "Think about it. Won't it be great to never be alone on a birthday or when you're sick? To have somebody who'll sleep with you even when you have a pimple on your nose?" he said.

"I never get pimples," she scoffed. She took a large gulp of her wine.

"Stop drinking the wine like that. It's a really special wine. You can't taste the flavour notes when you gulp down wine," he scolded her. "Roll it around on your tongue and think about what you're experiencing."

"Just because you're one of those wine snobs, doesn't mean everybody should be one." She took another slow sip. "I don't taste anything."

"I'm not a wine snob. I've learnt to appreciate beautiful things. You'll get it if you concentrate. Wait here." He got up and returned with a red tie. "Close your eyes," he ordered softly.

"Why? Are we going to play hide-and-seek?" asked Aditi amused.

"No." He took the glass of wine from her. "Sometimes you should just do what you're told, Aditi," said Sanjay.

She closed her eyes obediently. He wrapped the strip of silk around her eyes and brought the wine glass next to her nose.

"What do you smell?" he asked.

He was so close to her that Aditi was having a hard time smelling the wine. All she could smell was his warm, musky scent. "You."

"You're not concentrating on the wine," he said sternly, although he was secretly pleased. "The entire taste of a wine actually originates from its aroma. That's why people who appreciate wine like to sniff it first. Now smell it." He brought the wine close to her nose and let her sniff it. "Open your mouth."

He drizzled a few drops of wine on her tongue. "What do you taste?" he asked.

She concentrated on the liquid on her tongue. "Strawberries," she said in amazement.

"Very good," he said. He gave her another sip of wine. "What else?"

"Hmm…strawberries and some other berry. No. Wait. Cherries," exclaimed Aditi and took the blindfold off. His face was very close to hers and their gazes collided. Her eyes were shining with accomplishment. Understanding flashed between them. Aditi lowered her eyes. Goosebumps covered her arms. It was as if he had made love to her and he hadn't even touched her.

"Black currents. You're pretty close. That's the aroma of a Cabernet Sauvignon. The entire bouquet is a little more complex. We'll have an advanced class later. You're a wine snob now," he said teasingly. "Do you know the story behind this grape? It's very romantic."

"No. Tell me," she said quietly.

"Sometime in the 17th century, the Cabernet Franc, which is a red grape and the Sauvignon Blanc, which is a white grape, got married in the beautiful region of Bordeaux to produce this wonderful grape called the Cabernet Sauvignon. If two grapes could manage to put their differences aside to get together and give the world something so beautiful, why can't we?" murmured Sanjay.

Aditi had no answer to that. She just stared at him. Everything about him was always so cool. She took another sip of her wine and tried not to gulp.

RELATIONSHIP RULES

The next day, Aditi and Sanjay were sitting in Aditi's favourite Chinese restaurant. Both of them were scrutinizing the menu with intense concentration. Sanjay looked up from his menu and found Aditi looking at him. He smiled. She smiled back. He cleared his throat nervously. She looked at him expectantly. He went back to reading the menu.

What the hell was wrong with him, she thought to herself. Now that they had agreed to go out together he was barely talking to her. He hadn't even noticed the lovely white *salwar kameez* she was wearing.

"It's really hot today," he blurted out. He wondered why he had said that out loud. He had meant to say that she looked good in a *salwar kameez*, but it was made from some sheer white material and he could see right thorough it. The bodice was heavily embroidered and covered the essential bits of her but the rest of it was completely transparent and if he stared hard enough he could see her waist with its tiny little navel.

Aditi looked up from her menu and gave him a small smile. "It is quite pleasant," she said politely. This was not the way she had pictured their date. Sanjay was reading the menu as if his life depended on it.

"Have you thought about what to order?" he asked.

"Sure," she replied. It was a relief when the waiter came and took their order. "How about we order a starter, a main dish and some rice and we share?"

"Whatever," he said preoccupied. He picked up a file that he had brought with him and began to read it. He pinched his nose distractedly.

"So," he said after the waiter had left.

"So?" she asked puzzled.

"This is for you. My lawyer thought it would be a good idea to have this, just in case," he said searching her face and handing her the file that he was reading. Aditi looked at him bemused and opened the file. It looked like a legal document of some kind. She began to read.

She looked up astonished after a few minutes. "What's this?"

"It's a contract between us if anything goes wrong. Since you're not interested in marriage, my lawyer says we should have one. My old girlfriend took ten percent of my old company when she left me for my friend. I don't want to make any mistakes this time. It's always better when things are transparent from the start," said Sanjay matter-of-factly. "It protects you as much as me. Look it over. See…I've given up all claims over your assets and your dad's property."

She looked at the document. "Your ex-girlfriend left you for your friend and took ten percent of your company?" Aditi asked amazed. "She must be really smart." She took out a pen and signed the document.

"You didn't even read it properly," he protested.

"How bad can it be?" she said shrugging. "Atleast you're not lying to me to get me to sleep with you."

He looked at her surprised but didn't comment. "So how come someone as beautiful as you, isn't married yet? It's pretty unusual."

"I don't know. I just never met anybody I wanted to get married to," she said. She flipped the pages of the agreement and her eyes widened. "And what about you? Any past girlfriends?"

"Hmm…two. Both of them were named Sheetal. So just your name is making me pretty optimistic right now," he said. The waiter brought a plate of deep-fried lotus root in honey sauce. Sanjay automatically picked up a piece with a fork and brought it next to her mouth.

Aditi hesitated. Sanjay looked at her so she opened her mouth and took the bite into her mouth. Nobody had fed her since she was two-years old. She felt ridiculously pampered. "How did you meet them?" she asked interested.

"The first was nothing, a crush in college. The second Sheetal worked with me in my old company. Mayank, Jayshree, Sheetal and me used to all work in the same company. Sheetal quit along with me when I started my own company. She was one of my first employees, so I had promised her ten percent. I didn't realize it would become such a hassle later," he said shaking his head ruefully.

"I thought you sold your company. How come you're still tied to Sheetal?" she asked.

"I sold the controlling stock and resigned as CEO but Sheetal and I still have some stock left. Plus we have some property that we own jointly. My lawyers are sorting it out but it's taking a lot of time."

"Are you still in love with her?" she asked.

He remained silent. He was taken aback by Aditi's question. He didn't think Aditi quite grasped how complicated his relationship with Sheetal was. How exhausting it was. When you broke up with somebody after five years, they took a part of you with them, whether you still loved them or not. "It's not about being in love. We were together for five years. We lived together for two years when I bought a house. She was like family. I trusted her," he said finally.

"Then what happened?" she inquired. "Why did you two break up?"

"We got successful and took everything for granted. I was very preoccupied. She got bored and had an affair. The usual story…I don't really want to go into all the details," he said. "I'm more relaxed now. I want to do everything differently this time." He laughed self-consciously. "Atleast, that's the plan. I'm not sure if I can manage it."

"Well, having a contract is definitely different. You don't seriously think I'm going out with you for your money, do you?" she asked huskily. She tried not to be hurt but couldn't stop a little frisson of it bubbling up inside her. Why didn't anybody really fall in love anymore? It was always just about two people, their assets, their careers and their efforts to fit in each other's life. She was tired of being with guys who were just impressed with the image of her but never bothered to glance into her soul. Maybe this was Sanjay's way of dealing with superficial women. Still, she had thought that Sanjay and she were friends and he trusted her.

"No." He stopped for a moment to gather his thoughts.

"It's not that I don't trust you, Aditi. I just need this. Even if you did like me because I'm rich, I don't really care anymore. I would still go out with you. I get it, you know. Women are attracted to rich men. They are genetically programmed to find the best provider for their offspring and all that. I mean, you're beautiful. Men are biologically wired to be attracted to you because you'll have beautiful babies or whatever. But at the end of the day, you can't base a whole relationship on money or looks, can you? He took her hand in his. "I think we can really make this work. Isn't it better if things are totally clear from the start?"

Aditi had stopped listening to him after he started taking about babies. She drank some water to distract herself from the image of Sanjay and her making beautiful babies. She felt herself blushing. Why was she acting like a fifteen year-old? There was something about this guy with his stupid contract.

Sanjay leaned back in his chair and stared at the blush that spread across her face and neck and disappeared into the neckline of her dress. He wondered if it had spread further down. He really wanted to know. He tried guessing what she was thinking. Her face had gone from downcast to flaming red in five seconds. He never had so much difficulty in reading a person before. "What?" he asked.

"Nothing," she told him, smiling mysteriously.

"Anything else in the contract that bothers you?" he asked with a crooked smile. He was relieved that the awkward moment had passed.

"Hmm...There's a whole section on activities that both parties might wish to abstain from. Do you really need a contract for this? Can't we just discuss these things like adults?" said Aditi, her eyes twinkling. "And a section on not posting information and images on social media. Really? So I can't post a photo of us anywhere?"

Sanjay got flustered. He was going to kill Naveen, his lawyer. "Within reason. Sometimes some company information is confidential. When Sheetal and I broke up, the price of Paradigm stock fell by almost nine points. There was a loss of investor confidence. It's…" he trailed off when he saw Aditi's eyes glaze over. "I'll let you know if something is confidential. Don't worry about it."

"And it says here that you're willing to foot all the bills whenever we're together? That's very generous of you," she said laughing hard. "This is getting more and more interesting by the minute. Are you mad? Are you completely, totally insane? It's like I'm agreeing to be your mistress or something."

"Well," he said patiently. "You don't ever want to get married. So how do we define the relationship? There should be some basic rules, right? Can we date other people? For long are we going to be together? Have you really thought about this stuff? Because I need to know."

"No. We can't date other people. Isn't it obvious? I… but…," she said indecisively. "Okay fine. Have your stupid contract. By the way, I want to know when I can use the bathroom. Is that in the contract?"

Sanjay sighed and concentrated on the food on his plate. Aditi never really thought about anything completely. It was why her life was so chaotic. She hadn't even bothered to read the contract properly. He thought there were some very valid points in it. Complete honesty and fairness was the key to a successful relationship but Aditi was not in a mood to appreciate his point of view.

"Just forget the whole thing," he muttered. He should keep

his mouth shut as much as possible. He wished he had deleted the whole stupid contract. What was he thinking? These things didn't work in India. It had seemed so practical when Naveen had suggested it. Now he looked like a callous idiot. "Can I start over and talk about something pleasant? Mayank, Jayshree and I were thinking of going to this angel investor's conference in Phuket next month. Would you like to join us?" he asked.

"That sounds like fun. I'll speak to my parents and let you know for sure," said Aditi.

Suddenly Aditi grabbed Sanjay's hand tightly. "Shit! I have to get out of here. Do something. Anything," she said covering her face with the menu lying next to her. Nikhil had just walked in with his wife. She didn't want to go through all the drama of meeting him again.

Sanjay looked around him. "Why? What happened?" he asked puzzled. When he looked at Aditi, she had vanished. His cell phone rang.

"Hello?" he answered.

"Hi. It's me. I'm under the table," said Aditi over the phone.

"I can tell you're under the table. I can hear you. Come out. What is the matter with you? You haven't escaped from a mental institution, have you?" he asked confused. It would explain the strange way she behaved sometimes.

"No, you idiot. Do you see that man in the green shirt? He just walked in with that girl in the yellow blouse?" she asked from under the table.

Sanjay looked around the restaurant. He saw a tall, good-looking man seated in the corner along with a woman. "I saw him. Why are you hiding from him? And why are we talking on the phone? I can hear you even without it," he said disconnecting the phone.

"Hello! Hello!" she yelled from under the table.

"Stop yelling. It's bad enough that you're under the table. People will think we're doing something," he said embarrassed. Her hand was resting on his knee for support and it was not entirely an unpleasant sensation. He reluctantly adjusted his position to accommodate her more comfortably under the table. Her hand dropped from his knee and he began to miss it.

"What could I possibly be doing to you under the table," she said. "Oh! You have a dirty mind. I like it." She laughed.

"Will you come out? Why are you hiding from him?" He had heard of celebrities being stalked by fans and although Aditi was quite beautiful, she wasn't really that big of a celebrity and this man looked too normal to be a stalker. He was talking animatedly to the girl who was with him.

She thought about what to tell him. "He's my ex-boyfriend and he's with his wife," she said hurriedly. "Is it possible to leave? Do you think they saw us?"

Another ex-boyfriend? He bent and peered into her anxious face. "Why are you hiding from him?" he asked bemused. He debated about whether he should join her under the table. There didn't seem to be enough space for two people and that would probably look even worse.

"I didn't know that he was married when we were together. He didn't tell me that he was married. His wife was very upset when she found out. She called me a home-wrecker. I'm not a home-wrecker, Sanjay. I would never do that." Her light brown eyes became luminous and moist.

"Of course you won't. Come out, please. I look like I'm

talking to myself. You have nothing to be worried about. You didn't do anything wrong. He should be hiding under the table, not you," he told her.

"Can you please let me be here till they leave? I can still talk to you from under the table," she offered.

"As attractive as your offer sounds, I think I'll save it for another day. Now come out. This is ridiculous," he told her sternly.

Aditi slowly got out from under the table and took her seat at the table. "Can we at least pretend that we didn't notice them?" she asked him, smoothening her hair back into place.

"You know, there's never a dull moment with you. I have to give you that."

"You give all potential girlfriends a contract to sign and tell me there's never a dull moment with me? I'm so ordinary compared to you," she replied. Sanjay fed her a piece of mushroom. Her mouth opened automatically. She wondered if she'll ever be able to eat by herself again. "It'll be really fun to go to Phuket with Mayank and Shree. Thanks for asking. And by the way, I'll pay for my own ticket. I know you said you'll pay for everything, but it's really not necessary with me. I have my own money. Do we split the room?"

Sanjay's was embarrassed. "There's no need, Aditi. I'm a speaker. The room's included. If you would like your own room, that's fine too. And I'll book everything. I can afford it. If we were married, this wouldn't be an issue at all. Then why should it be a problem when you're my girlfriend?" he grumbled. He wished he had never brought the contract with him. He was getting bored of this discussion. He had ruined a perfectly good evening.

"I'm not your girlfriend. You haven't even said that you loved me yet," she said.

"I don't believe in all that nonsense," he said gruffly. "I would marry you right now. You're the one who doesn't want anything serious." He signed the credit card slip that the waiter placed before him and put his card back into his wallet. "Ready to leave?"

"Sure. But I don't feel like going back home just yet. Is there somewhere else we could go?" she asked moodily. "Can we go to your place and play the wine game?"

"It's not a wine game. I was teaching you to appreciate wine," he protested.

"Whatever. It was fun," she said.

"If we do that again, I'm not responsible for what happens after it," he said cheerfully. "I know a great place where we can go. Let's go."

"Somewhere dark and quiet, I bet," she said looking into his eyes. She could get used to looking into his eyes.

"You know me so well already, Aditi." He took her hand. He had never been much of a hand-holder, but he liked holding Aditi's hand. It almost drowned in his hand.

Half an hour later, they were whizzing by the desolate landscape that surrounded the Outer Ring Road. Sanjay slowed down the car at an exit and took a small dirt road that lead to a hidden lake. It was almost eleven at night and the only sign of life was the occasional cars that were going to the airport. He stopped the car at the end of the dirt road and got out. "Isn't this place great?" he said enthusiastically.

"I pass by this place so often on my way to the airport but I've never noticed this. It's kind of scary out here in the night," she said, slowly getting out of the car. After looking around, she had to admit it was quite a romantic spot. The little lake was nestled between huge boulders and moonlight reflected off the water. Even though there seemed to be a small cluster of houses and shops nearby, the only sound that could be heard was of the crickets and the waves gently lapping the edge of the lake.

He changed the song playing on the music system. Timbaland crooned softly in the background. "Do you want to have some tea? There's a tea shop a bit further down this path and it looks like it's still open."

"Sounds great," she said as she climbed on the hood and leaned on the windshield while he trudged down towards the tea shop. White, cotton-candy clouds dotted the sky and a few scattered stars peeped out from behind them. A slight breeze was blowing and it was cool without being too cold. Aditi felt all the tension of meeting Nikhil in the restaurant melting away from her body as she watched the water. Sanjay handed her the tea in a tiny plastic cup and stood next to her drinking his own.

She leaned over and kissed him impulsively on the cheek. He finished his tea and looked at her. He thought briefly of Sheetal and cursed himself. It wasn't as if he was cheating on Sheetal. Sheetal had cheated on him more than a year ago. Why was he thinking of her now? He came closer and leaned over her. He brushed the hair off her face. His face came close to hers and his lips brushed the corner of her mouth and moved towards her jaw.

"Is this in the contract? Would your lawyer approve?" asked Aditi huskily. Her heart was beginning to pound loudly and she wondered if he could hear.

"Didn't you read section 21B on quality and frequency of physical intimacy," he whispered against her ear. Aditi tensed.

He laughed softly. "I'm joking, Aditi." He planted soft kisses in a straight line from her ear to her shoulder. Aditi closed her eyes. Her fingers came up and tangled in his hair. She lifted her face to meet his lips. His hands tightened around her waist as he deepened the kiss and pushed her against the car.

He drew away and looked at Aditi's face. Her eyes were still closed. When she opened them, she looked suitably dazed and dreamy. A million times better than any kiss he shared with Sheetal, he thought with satisfaction. He gave himself a mental high-five. He kissed her again just to make sure it wasn't a fluke. It wasn't. "Come home with me. No. Let's go to a hotel," he said shakily.

"I can't go to a hotel with some strange guy. People know me around here," she said, smiling. You have a perfectly fine car right here, if you're so inclined."

He looked at the car doubtfully. "You can't go to a comfortable hotel but you don't mind doing it in a car? I don't want our first time to be like that. You don't just glug down a Cristal straight from the bottle. It's the whole experience that's important." He stroked her cheek. "But thanks for the offer. You seem quite eager."

"Stop smirking. You're ruining everything," she told him mock angrily and leaned against the windshield, a smile curving her lips. Did he just compare her to fine Champagne? He'd made her feel like fine Champagne. She now knew what a Champagne bottle felt like when it had just been opened. Light and frothy.

FOUR IS A CROWD

Jayshree opened the door to the balcony to get a better view of the Andaman Sea. They had just checked in at the *Holiday Inn Resort* in Phuket. She had inspected the bathroom with its fluffy towels and toiletries, the coffee maker and the mini bar and was now checking out the ocean view from their room.

When Sanjay had told them that Aditi would be joining them, she had been so excited. It was so much fun to have another couple around and Sanjay and Aditi got along so well with her and Mayank. She hoped Aditi had the good sense to stick around with Sanjay. He was so perfect for Aditi. Calm and controlled in comparision to Aditi's vivaciousness and exuberance.

"This is so great, Mayank." She beamed at him as he stepped into the balcony. It had been more than a year since they had gone on a vacation. Most of her holidays now comprised of either visiting her parents in Chennai or attending weddings of assorted relatives in different cities. She turned to Mayank who was seated on the cane chairs placed in the balcony with his feet up on the coffee table in front of him and his palms behind his head. "Promise me there's going to be no pregnancy talk during the conference," she said solemnly.

"No talk about pregnancy during the conference," he promised.

"Then why were you reading a book called 'How to be a dad?' on the plane," she demanded. "You think you can learn to be dad by reading a hundred-pages book?"

"There no harm on doing some research in advance. Do you know how many websites and apps there are about conception and pregnancy?" he asked. "You can just type in the date of your last period and they tell you when to do it."

"If you ever use any of those apps on me, you'll be doing it to yourself for a really long time. Okay?" she threatened. "Should we go and check on what Aditi and Sanjay are doing?" she asked.

"They aren't babies that we should check on them all the time." He got up and put his arms around his wife. "You checked out everything in the room. Why don't we try out the bed too?" he murmured.

"But you just promised. No trying for a baby while we are at the conference," she protested.

"I know," he said. "This isn't to get pregnant. This is just for fun."

Jayshree smiled. "There's a difference?" she enquired.

"Of course there's a difference," he said.

In the next room, Sanjay was standing and talking to the conference organizers on his phone with one hand stuck into the pocket of his jeans. Seeing that he was busy with work, Aditi had gathered up her hair into a bun and collapsed on the bed with her laptop. She squinted manfully into the screen trying to squeeze some words out of her brain. It was a relief when the bellhop entered the room with their bags and distracted her. Aditi watched with embarrassment as the small-built man struggled to place her enormous suitcase on the luggage rack.

Sanjay looked at him with pity. He tipped the bellhop generously and sent him on his way and lifted Aditi's suitcase effortlessly onto the rack without skipping even a second of his phone conversion. He went back to leaning against the wall. Aditi gaped inwardly. That was the hottest and the coolest thing she had ever seen any man do.

Sanjay finished his conversation and came and sat on the bed next to Aditi. He released her hair from her bun and she turned around to smile at him. "What are you doing?" he asked.

She rolled to the side to give him space on the bed and he stretched out on the bed beside her. She snuggled into his chest and his arms automatically wrapped around her like they had been doing it for years. "I'm trying to make sense of my novel. You want to read some of it and give me your opinion?" She untangled herself from his limbs and handed her laptop to him. He sat up and began to read.

Aditi tried to gauge his reaction from his facial expressions, but except for a slightly raised eyebrow, he didn't give much away. He scrolled down the pages at a brisk speed. "You can't possibly be reading that fast," she protested.

"I read fast," he said annoyed. "And there's not much matter to make it difficult. Are you writing the story around the intimate scenes or the scenes around the story?"

She flushed guiltily. "Is it that bad?"

He softened and struggled to be diplomatic. "No. But

there's not much of a plot." He looked at her appraisingly. "Hmm...If you could write this book anyway you liked without interference then would you write it differently?"

"Probably," she said uncertainly.

He frowned. "Then why don't you write the kind of book you want to write and change publishers?"

She thought about what he said and made a face. Then she buried her face in his arm again. "I would have to scrap this whole book and start all over. That's six months of my life wasted," she mumbled against his arm.

"So do it. It's better to lose six months and learn something from it than to keep making the same mistake forever," he said as she made herself more comfortable against his body. He looked down at her moulding herself around him and smiled. "Aditi, have you done this before?"

"Written a book? You know I have." She looked up at him puzzled.

"No. I mean gone on a vacation with someone before," he asked seriously. He didn't have to explain what he meant by 'someone'.

"No, I haven't."

He felt relieved but he forced himself not to read too much into it. The fact that Aditi hadn't gone on a vacation with any other guy before didn't particularly mean she was getting serious about him. She buried herself deeper into his chest. He looked at Aditi's unresponsive form. Aditi had fallen asleep on his arm and was drooling on him to boot. He kept her laptop aside and watched her sleeping. After a few minutes, he was dozing himself.

They woke up to the sound of pounding on their door.

"Hey. We are going swimming. Do you guys want to join?" Mayank was shouting from behind the door.

Aditi stirred in Sanjay's arms and noticed the wet patch on his shirt. "Oh my God. I'm so sorry." She exclaimed clapping her hand over her mouth. She disappeared into the bathroom as Sanjay answered the door.

Sanjay spoke briefly with Mayank and shut the door. He turned towards Aditi who had re-emerged from the bathroom. Aditi stood before him wearing a bikini. "What the hell are you wearing? Are you going to walk around the hotel wearing that?" he demanded grumpily.

"Everybody out here is dressed like this. What's the big deal? I don't work out for an hour every day so that I can wear a burqua," she said. She tied a sarong around her waist.

"You're going to swim in that," he protested weakly. He didn't want to know what her outfit would look like when it was wet. Actually, a small part of him did, but mostly he didn't.

"I'm not going to swim. I don't know how to. I'll just sit by the pool. Don't tell me what I can or can't wear. I don't like that. Are you coming or should I go alone?" she said annoyed.

Sanjay was confused about what to do. He should have had a small clause about appropriate clothing in the agreement. He didn't want to start their vacation with a fight but he just couldn't imagine walking casually in public with a half-naked Aditi. "Can you please atleast put a shirt on? To make me happy?" he asked her nicely.

Aditi glared at him and then sighed. "Okay. I'll put a shirt on," she said reluctantly. She took out a tank top from her suitcase and put it on. He gave up. "Are all your clothes like this?" he asked resigned. He wondered why she needed such a big suitcase when all her clothes were so tiny.

"It's a beach resort, Sunny. Everybody here is dressed like this," she said soothingly. "You'll get used to it in a day or two. Are you sure you used to live in the US and not in Afganistan?"

"Funny," he said. "And I told you not to call me Sunny."

When they were near the pool, Sanjay dived cleanly into the pool while Aditi settled on a bamboo chaise longue and placed a huge pair of sunglasses on her nose. She had just opened the book she had brought with her when a shadow fell across her. She looked up to see Sharad grinning at her. She took off her sunglasses and squealed in delight.

Sanjay was talking to Mayank when he heard Aditi. He turned to see what had amused her so much and stopped mid-sentence when he saw Sharad sitting on the chair next to Aditi's, laughing merrily along with her. They both looked like they belonged in an ad for a beach resort, he thought unhappily, noting their matching sunglasses. Sharad offered Aditi his bottle of beer and Aditi took a polite sip. If he offered Aditi another sip, he would break the bottle on Sharad's head, Sanjay vowed furiously then turned back to Mayank who was watching him interestedly.

"Maybe you should go and beat him up. You look like you want to," said Mayank trying to hide a smile.

"I'm glad you find it so amusing," said Sanjay smiling back.

"I've not seen you like this. Not even with Sheetal," smirked Mayank.

"Sheetal was not idiotic like Aditi," Sanjay replied.

"Sheetal was not hot like Aditi and not nearly as charming," said Mayank. "Get used to it. It's going to happen often."

Jayshree swam up to the two of them. "A little drama going on, I see." She smiled wistfully. "Enjoy it when you can. After you guys get married, you'll start to miss it."

Mayank frowned at her. "You don't think there's enough drama in our lives."

She made a face at him. "Not the good kind."

"Why do you think Aditi and I are getting married? She still hasn't changed her mind," said Sanjay bleakly. He couldn't believe just a short while ago she was wrapped around him like she couldn't get enough of him.

"So what exactly were you thinking when you asked her out? Aditi is not getting married anytime soon unless you drag her to the mantap kicking and screaming," said Mayank.

Jayshree glared at Mayank. "You will definitely get married to Aditi, Sanjay. Anybody who sees the two of you together can tell that Aditi is ready for something more."

"Oh? So what would the next level be for Aditi?" mused Sanjay.

"Right now, I think it's a threesome," murmured Mayank chuckling.

"Mayank," scolded Jayshree. "Don't pay attention to him. It's not true. Aditi's not like that at all." She turned to Mayank. "I think I'll go back to the room. I feel a little dizzy."

"What happened?" asked Mayank concerned.

"Nothing. Maybe the sun," said Jayshree getting out of the water. Mayank followed her.

Sanjay got out of the water and reluctantly walked upto Sharad and Aditi, snagging a towel from the counter on the way. "Hi Sharad. How have you been?" he asked politely. "What are you doing in Phuket?"

"I'm getting some pre-fabricated materials shipped from Bangkok. I stopped for a couple of days in Phuket to chill," he said casually. "Meeting you guys here is an unexpected bonus. You and Aditi. I never would have guessed," he said heartily patting Sanjay on the back. "You make a great couple."

Sanjay thawed a little after hearing the whole-hearted approval in Sharad's voice. "I'll head upstairs, Aditi. I want to take a shower. See you around, Sharad." He left them near the pool, cracking jokes and laughing together. He still wasn't totally convinced about Aditi hanging around Sharad, but atleast he didn't feel like murdering Sharad anymore.

By the time Aditi came back to the room, Sanjay had showered and changed and was playing chess on his laptop. Aditi came and settled into his lap. "What's so interesting on your laptop?"

Sanjay leaned back and grinned. He ran his hand from her heel to her knee to her thigh. "You're a much better laptop. What's so interesting about Sharad?"

Aditi sighed. "I told you. He's just a friend. Why do you keep thinking about him?"

"He makes you laugh in a way I don't know how to," he said anxiously. "You're never like that with me. All happy and relaxed."

"Do you know why I don't feel relaxed when I'm with you?" she asked seriously. He shook his head. "Because this is not funny…" She buried her fingers in his hair and lowered her head to his. They were both a little breathless when they broke apart a few minutes later. Aditi eyes were shining when she looked into his. He looked at her skimpy outfit and thanked God. He must have been a celibate saint in his previous life to deserve Aditi. He carried her to the bed and lowered her carefully to the bed. "You're so light," he whispered. He got in beside her and kissed her again. He lowered the straps of her top and Aditi took off his T-shirt.

They were startled when someone knocked on their door. Mayank shouted out from behind the door. "Hey! You guys. We have some good news. We think Jayshree might be pregnant."

Sanjay rolled away from Aditi and cursed under his breath. "I knew it was a mistake to come with Mayank. Everything is always about him. Idiot." He sat on the edge of the bed with his elbows on his thighs and forced himself to think about how much money he had lost in the Tyler-Boone Corporation scandal last year. His heart rate and other body parts began to normalize. He put on his T-shirt. He looked at Aditi adjusting her clothes and smiled at her apologetically. He made his way towards the door and Aditi followed.

Mayank and Jayshree stood outside their door, their faces bright with excitement. Aditi hugged Mayank and then hugged Jayshree tightly. "Congrats. You must be so happy, Shree."

"Great news, man," said Sanjay patting Mayank on the shoulder. He wondered when he was going to have kids. Most likely, when he was really, really old. Aditi was the only woman in the world without a biological clock.

WHAT HAPPENS IN PHUKET

"**M**ayank, what are we doing?" asked Jayshree as she stirred the *Tom Yum Kung* that she was making. Mayank was adding the fish sauce to his shrimp soup. They were taking a cookery class that the hotel had organized.

"What do you mean, what are we doing?" he asked taking a look at the recipe that was handed to all of them. "We're learning to make *Tom Yum Kung*."

"Why? Everybody else is having a good time boozing, shopping and watching pole-dancers. Why are we cooking?" she wanted to know.

"Because both of us like to cook. Don't you want to do this?" he asked puzzled.

"The smell is making me nauseous. Why can't we just do things that are fun? Like that day we bunked work," she pleaded.

"If there is something else you want to do, why don't you just tell me instead of talking in riddles?" he told her in frustration. Jayshree was just getting impossible to please. He didn't know what he could do to make things better. The harder he tried, the unhappier she seemed. He wondered anxiously if they were going through the famous seven-year-itch. He looked at her and softened. She was pregnant now. He should be more patient.

"Can we go for a walk on the beach," she asked softly.

"Sure," he said surprised. "I'm almost done with my soup. Can you wait for five minutes?"

"Fine," she replied.

When they reached the beach, the sun was about to set. The sky had a lovely pink cast and the deep orange sun highlighted the fluffy grey clouds. Jayshree sat on the sand. Mayank sat next to her and looked at her expectantly.

"What's wrong?" he asked seriously.

"Nothing's wrong," she said making circles in the sand.

"Something is wrong. You're not happy. You haven't been for a long time and I don't know how to fix it," he said sadly.

"I don't know how to fix it either," she replied. She really didn't. She didn't want to behave like a drama queen all the time. She knew she was hurting Mayank and that was the last thing she wanted to do. "I think I want to go back to the US," she said finally. "And before you say anything, just think about it. Put your family and work aside for a minute. Weren't we happier and more relaxed there?"

Mayank was quiet for a long time. "I think your romanticizing our life in the States a bit. We had pretty much this same life out there too. We fought about the same things. The pressure was the same. I admit my mother is more annoying in the flesh than on the phone, but then it's not like we live with her, so what's the real problem?"

"There's always this feeling that nothing exciting is ever going to happen to me anymore. Look at Aditi. Our circumstances are not that different but her life is completely different from mine. When we have this baby, it's going to be even worse. It's like I'm stuck in a rut," she said. She didn't know how to explain to him how envious she felt about Aditi's casual approach to life. She picked up men and dropped men. Did whatever she wanted. Went wherever she wanted. Whenever she wanted. Nothing ever held her back.

"We're going to have a baby and you're saying nothing exciting is ever going to happen to you anymore? Of course her life is different from yours. You're married, she's not," he said.

"The baby is only going to make it worse. There's nothing romantic about our relationship any more, Mayank. You're the only guy I ever kissed or slept with and it's only going to be you forever. There's nothing more to look forward to. No pounding heart, no first kiss, nothing. Just vomit, pee and poop," she complained.

"This is your big problem? What do you want me to do about it? Give you permission to have an affair before the baby comes?" he said irritably. "You want something different and exciting in our relationship but you're scared of going forward. Having kids is the next step in our life. I don't know why you can't see that. We can't go back to how we were. That's never going to happen," he said standing up and dusting sand from his trousers. "I can't help you with this. You have to sort out your own head."

Tears pricked her eyes. Mayank would never understand what she was feeling. It was so easy to explain things to Aditi. Maybe he was right. This wasn't about the two of them. It was about her. Even marriage has its limitations.

"Are you coming?" he asked when she didn't stand up.

"I think I'll sit here for a while," she said.

He strode out towards the ocean without saying a word. She could tell that she had made him angry, but she was glad she had talked to him. He was wading in the water and his trousers were getting wet. He finally sat down on the wet sand at the water's edge. She wanted to call out to him about his wet clothes, but stopped herself. He was right. Everything wasn't always about the two of them. His wet clothes were his problem, not hers. That's how Aditi would handle it, she thought. Aditi would also take action, instead of moaning and groaning about her problems.

When he came back, he was soaking wet and the sky had gone dark. His clothes were clinging to his body. His shoulders were broader now than when they were first married, she noticed. His face had filled out and the boyish look had gone. He had also developed a tan since coming to India. When had all that happened? How can you be married to somebody for seven years and not notice that they had changed? Suddenly it dawned on her. When you're single, you have the liberty to fall in and out of love as you pleased. The trick to keep a marriage working was to fall in love with the same person every time life changed. It would always be the same person. It was the changing circumstances that would make it exciting. She stood up when he came near.

"Ready to leave?" he asked his face unreadable.

She put her arms around his shoulders and kissed him hungrily before she lost her nerve. He froze for a minute and then responded. His lips softened on hers and his arms came around to hold her. It felt good to take the lead instead of always following his cue, she thought.

"I'm getting you wet," he said when they broke away.

"Yes, you are," she replied huskily.

He smiled at his unintended double entendre. "We should go," he murmured kissing her again and pulling her close.

"Let's do it here. It's dark now and nobody's around," she said boldly looking in his eyes. There was never a problem in this department. It was the only time he was totally hers and she wasn't sharing him with his parents or friends or employees. She ran her hands under his shirt.

"Why?" he asked puzzled.

"Because I want to do it here," she said before taking her top off.

He inhaled deeply and looked around worriedly to see if anybody was around. He led her behind some rocks where there was some privacy. "Shree, this is crazy. What's wrong with you?" he asked as she lay him down and took off his wet shirt. "And how come you get to be on top?"

"Are you kidding? I'm pregnant. Do you want me to get hurt?" she panted as she took off her jeans and perched on top of him.

"The baby, Shree?" he asked worriedly, suddenly remembering.

"Nothing is going to happen to the baby. We'll never be able to do this after the baby comes. Make the most of the time we have," There was no more talk after that and Mayank no longer bothered about the baby and who was watching.

Blissfully unaware of their friends' personal drama, Aditi and Sanjay were strolling along Patong Beach. Aditi hadn't bought anything yet. She spotted a stall selling swimwear.

"Do you think this will look good on me?" She held a minuscule, yellow bikini top against her chest trying to irritate Sanjay. Or seduce him. She was never quite sure what she wanted to do to him.

"Everything looks good on you," said Sanjay diplomatically. They were strolling aimlessly for almost two hours and Aditi still hadn't found anything she liked. He was getting bored. She abandoned the bikini and walked out of the store.

"Are you really going to buy anything or are you just trying to pass time. There are plenty of more exciting things to do if you don't want to buy anything," said Sanjay.

"I don't know. I don't really like anything," she replied.

"Then what have we been during for the past two hours? Let's get out of here," he ordered. "There's a Starbucks down the road. Do you want to have some coffee?"

"Coffee? I didn't come to Phuket to have coffee. Let's go for a drink," she demanded.

They strolled down the road following the music till it reached deafening levels as they reached Bangla Street. People of all race and gender could be found staring in awe at the neon lights, 'lady boys' and the dancers in the Go-Go bars. If there was ever a place on earth where raunchiness was celebrated in total abandonment, this was it. Even Aditi was a bit overwhelmed with the sight.

"Isn't this place fabulous? Let's go inside that place it seems to be really happening," she said excitedly pointing to sign that claimed to be Oscar Bar on Soi Tiger.

"Are you sure this is where you want to go," he asked uncertainly eyeing the five girls in bikinis who were gyrating around poles. "There are some nice places back there that are quieter."

"Of course I want to go here," she said plonking herself at a table as a bar-girl came and handed them a drink's menu. "So aren't you going to ask them to cover up?" she asked him cheekily. He ignored her. Aditi ordered a mojito while Sanjay ordered a Thai wine.

"You're having wine in Thailand?"

He shrugged. "They make a great Malaga Blanc here. They have these floating vineyards near Bangkok where they grow grapes," he replied. "We should have gone there. I wish we had planned this trip properly." He tucked a strand of her hair behind her ear.

When their drinks and food arrived, Sanjay offered his wine to Aditi to taste. She took a tentative sip of the wine. "Aren't you going to blindfold me?" she asked.

"A blindfold is not a normal part of drinking wine, Aditi," he said, feeding her a piece of *calamari* and popping another into his mouth.

"But it definitely makes it kinkier," she said. "Did you play the wine game with Sheetal?"

"It's not a wine game. I just wanted you to experience all the flavours. You can do that better if your eyes are closed," said Sanjay exasperated. "And no, I didn't play the wine game, as you call it, with Sheetal. It was just a spontaneous thing, not some cheesy move I make on all girls."

Aditi felt glad. She didn't want to think that he had shared something like that with Sheetal. "And did you feed her too?"

Sanjay looked embarrassed. "Sheetal didn't like it, so I stopped. She said it made her feel like a pet dog. Why all these questions about Sheetal?"

Aditi shrugged. Affection made Sheetal feel like a pet dog?

What kind of crazy woman was she? "I just wanted to know what she was like. I know she was smart. Was she pretty too?"

He looked into his drink. "After a while, it stops being about how a person looks and becomes more about how a person makes you feel," he said. "Sheetal understood my way of thinking. We had an intellectual connection. Anyway, she's in Phuket for the conference. I'm sure you'll bump into her one of these days. Then you can see for yourself."

Aditi processed this new piece of information. Intellectual Sheetal who understood his way of thinking was here in Phuket. She could be intellectual if she put her mind to it too. She searched for something interesting to say. "So do you think Facebook stealing Paul Adams away from Google is going to hurt Google much?" she asked nonchalantly.

"Huh?" he looked at her surprised at her sudden change of topic. "Well, Paul Adams is more of a social scientist. His skill set suits Facebook better than Google. Google is still primarily an engineering company, so as a researcher he probably felt his voice was not being heard," he said warming to the topic. "It's very interesting. You can read his blog….."

"Er…Sanjay. I don't really know who Paul Adams is," she confessed. "I was just trying to get you to talk. I read that line in the magazine you were reading in the plane."

"You don't have pretend to be something you're not to impress me," he said, touched that she had gone through so much trouble. "I already like you. You're pretty amazing." He took her hand and stroked her knuckles with his thumb.

She was somewhat mollified, but the intellectual bit still bugged her. Did he think she wouldn't understand him? "How do I make you feel, Sanjay?" she persisted. She was quite certain there was nothing intellectual about it.

Sanjay tried to think of how Aditi made him feel. He shot her a pleading look but she didn't look like she was going to let it slide. "I know what you want me to say. It's not going to happen. I'm not that kind of guy," he said apologetically.

"Nonsense. Anybody can be that kind of guy. Come on. Don't think. Just feel," she coaxed. Sanjay looked liked he would rather face a firing squad. His face had turned a greenish grey.

"You make me crazy," he said while Aditi was squeezing his hand encouragingly. Crazy didn't quite cover it, he thought. He struggled to articulate. "Sometimes you're light like chardonnay, sometimes intense like a vintage port." He looked at Aditi to see if she was following him. She was just staring at him. "Somebody could dust you with powdered sugar and place you in a bakery with all the other pretty cakes and you'd fit right in." He laughed softly at the image. What the hell was he saying?

Aditi thought that he was done. He wasn't. "We're different but we go well together…like bread and butter," he said, looking at her.

"And you thought you weren't romantic," she said breathily. She was flattered that he had compared her to food and wine. They were very high up on his list of favourite things. A simple 'I love you' would have been too trite for him.

"Are you going to let me keep any of my dignity or do you want me to ramble on some more?" he asked. It suddenly felt too noisy and crowded in the bar and he was feeling weird. "Do you want to go back?"

"Umm…okay," she said as they stood up. She looked at Sanjay. He was looking at her like she was his favourite pastry. She linked her arm in his as they walked. "I love you," she said softly.

MEETING THE ENEMY

Aditi got up in the morning with a smile on her face. Too bad Sanjay had already woken up and was taking a shower. She had some interesting ideas about what they could do together. He came out of the bathroom with damp hair and a towel wrapped around his waist. He looked unbearably cute, she thought.

"Hey! You're up," he said smiling. He took out a dark grey suit, white shirt and silver tie from his suitcase. She was just wondering if he needed some privacy to dress when he took the towel off to wear his slacks. Apparently not. She always marvelled at how supremely confident men were about their bodies. Even the bald, beer-bellied ones were studs in their own mind. Women on the other hand, obsessed over each microscopic flaw as if they were the Hunchback of Notre-Dame. She had seen Sujaya going crazy about a pimple for days.

"Aren't you planning on getting up?" he said coming and sitting on the bed. His shirt was unbuttoned, his hair was uncombed and he smelled of soap. Her stomach fluttered.

"Oh God! Just do it," she murmured pulling him closer

to her and brushing his lips with hers. He didn't need much encouragement to take it further. "You know I've dreamed of this...that we'll be rolling around in white sheets. Dreams do come true."

He gave her an affectionate peck on the nose and got up. "There's no time to roll around now," he said ruefully.

"Are you still planning on going to the conference?" she asked, feeling bereft.

"Of course. I'm a speaker." He buttoned his shirt and knotted his tie. "Shit, it's really late."

"Aren't we having breakfast together?" she asked.

"There'll be something to eat at the conference. I'm already late. I have to leave," he said apologetically. "We'll have dinner together." He sat on the bed and opened his laptop bag and began checking some papers. Aditi scrambled upto him to see what he was doing.

"I keep forgetting you're a doctor," she asked reading the conference schedule. She put her arms around his neck. It was like he was doused with some addictive drug and she couldn't get enough, she thought crossly. "So, tell me what's wrong with me?"

"That might take a long time," he said laughing. "Anyway, I'm a Ph.D. not a medical doctor." He gently peeled her arms off from around his neck and rose to fetch his socks and shoes. "Have fun! I should be free by about five," he said, grabbing his coat and rushing out.

Yeah. Have fun. Mayank, Jayshree and Sanjay would all be at the conference. And probably Sheetal too. How was she supposed to have fun knowing that, she fumed. She picked up his clothes that he had abandoned on the floor and hung it in the closet. Did he think she was going to pick up after him? That part wasn't in the agreement. Some of his clean clothes were lying in an untidy mess on top of his suitcase. She folded them and opened his suitcase to put them back in. She didn't feel like going out without Sanjay so she decided to spend the rest of the day reworking her book.

She worked non-stop, pausing only to have a quick sandwich at lunch time. By five, she was tired and eager to see Sanjay again. His conference must be over by now, she thought impatiently. She decided to meet him downstairs instead of waiting for him to come to the room. She opened her suitcase to choose an outfit. If Sheetal was hanging around him, she wanted to look her best. Ever since she had started going around with Sanjay, she had become careless about what she wore and didn't even wear make-up around him. He cribbed if her mascara rubbed off on him and had once claimed that her lipstick tasted like a wax candle so she had stopped wearing both. He never seemed to care what she wore so she had stopped dressing up. But not tonight.

It would be dinner time soon so she wore her green sleeveless Donna Karan dress and her highest heels. The knee-length dress was modest enough not to give him a heart attack but tight enough to raise his blood pressure a little, she thought gleefully. That was another advantage of being with Sanjay. She could wear her highest heels and he would still be taller than her. She went down and looked for Sanjay and found him in the coffee shop with two other men and a woman in black slacks and a white shirt. Something in the way that Sanjay spoke to her told Aditi that the woman was Sheetal.

Looking at Sheetal was a bit of a let-down. She was of average height and slightly plump, but she had a pretty face.

Her sandals didn't really match with her outfit which was obviously a designer one. She had worried for nothing.

She walked up to Sanjay purposefully. He smiled at her when she approached, his eyes crinkling in the corner in a way that she found adorable. The other two men stood up to greet her. One of them stumbled when he tried to offer her his chair. The other just stared at her. She had that effect on men before. She was happy she hadn't lost it. Another chair was pulled up and all were seated again. She turned to Sheetal and looked into a pair of amused eyes. I know you bimbo types and I can deal with you, her eyes seemed to say. I don't really care, she tried to tell Sheetal with hers.

One of the men smiled broadly. "You look very familiar, actually. Have we met before?" he asked leaning towards Aditi. Sanjay looked at Ganesh surprised. Even he knew that was the oldest line in the book. He gritted his teeth. He wished Aditi would blend inconspicuously into the background for atleast a few moments each day, so that he could concentrate on other aspects of his life once in a while.

Aditi was prepared. "Maybe you saw me in a porn video," she said, making Ganesh blush a deep red.

"She's just joking. Aditi has a weird sense of humour," said Sanjay hastily. "Aditi, meet Ganesh Reddy, he used to be in charge of a hedge fund in Goldman Sachs and now has his own venture capital firm, Veritas Ventures and Neeraj Jain of Indigo Networks. They've come down from the US. And this is Sheetal Puri. Sheetal and me used to work together," said Sanjay. "Everybody, this is Aditi. Aditi is a writer."

"So you don't do porn videos?" asked Ganesh. He looked slightly disappointed. "What kind of books do you write?"

"Mainly romances," she replied.

"That's interesting. We get stuck meeting the same type of people all the time. I've never met a writer before. So how do you get your story ideas?" asked Neeraj enthusiastically.

"By harassing total strangers into telling her their love stories," piped in Sanjay casually draping his arm around her chair and leaning towards her. She felt secretly thrilled as she knew that it was the closest thing to a public display of affection that Sanjay would ever indulge in.

It did not thrill Sheetal. Her lips tightened. "So Sanjay, I heard your webpage is picking up."

"There are still some bugs to fix. It's kind of catching on. I wasn't really expecting it," said Sanjay modestly.

"You should promote it at the conference. You know how big something can get if you do the right advertising," she said excitedly.

"Promote it?" Sanjay frowned. "Aditi wants me to shut it down. She says guys are using the software to stalk girls."

"Any networking site can be misused. It doesn't make it wrong. Is Aditi an expert in business?" asked Sheetal, her eyes shining with some unfathomable emotion. "You could atleast try."

Sanjay just looked at Sheetal steadily. He leaned closer to Aditi. "If Aditi says something is not right, I trust her judgement."

Aditi clenched her jaw tightly, trying to stifle a yawn. Now she knew what Sanjay had meant by intellectual relationship. All they did was talk about technology, new products on the market and better investment options. No wonder Sheetal had run off at the first opportunity. She wondered if Sanjay realized what a bore he could be sometimes. "I think I'll go check out the shops. Do you want to join me in the shopping area outside in about half an hour?" she asked Sanjay.

"Wait! I'm pretty much done too. Why don't you have some coffee?" he offered.

"You carry on. I'll see you later," she said gently. "Bye Sheetal. It was nice meeting you," she said smiling at the other woman. A lull in the conversation followed Aditi's departure and Neeraj excused himself. Ganesh followed soon after.

Sanjay felt awkward sitting with Sheetal when he should have left with Aditi. Sheetal wasn't really a part of his life anymore and he wanted to be with Aditi. She had been quite mature about meeting Sheetal. He smiled unconsciously when he thought about her walking away in her high heels. She looked as great from behind as she did from the front.

"So you're with Aditi now?" Sheetal asked Sanjay with amazement as soon as Aditi was out of earshot. "What are you doing Sanjay? Since when did you start liking the Page 3, socialite types?"

"What do you mean?" he said. "Aditi's very nice. We have a great time together."

"No. I get it. You just met her. She's gorgeous. It must be really fun to be with her right now. But what will you talk about five or ten years down the line? Can you really see yourself settling down with her?" she asked. She wondered how Sanjay had changed so much.

"Of course. We have a lot in common. We can talk about anything. It was rough the first few months when I went back to India, but everything has fallen into place since I met her. I bought a house, met all my old friends. It's all working out good." He didn't mention that Aditi was totally against getting married and he had temporarily put all his grand marriage plans on hold.

"I think you're on the rebound Sanjay. Believe me I get why you're with her right now. It must be like a breath of fresh air after us. Everything about us was always so intense. But I made a huge mistake. You have to give us another chance. We were together for five years. That means something. I'm so sorry I totally messed everything up," she said passionately.

"We were not intense, Sheetal," said Sanjay. "If we were really so intense, you would have discussed how you felt with me, not had an affair with Naresh. See, Aditi would never do that. If she was not happy with me, she would leave me, not pretend to be my devoted girlfriend while having a discreet little affair behind my back."

"Why would I leave? Why should I give up something that I helped you build? You couldn't have done it without me, Sanjay," said Sheetal.

Sanjay stared at her in disbelief. "I know you've helped me, but don't be under the delusion that I couldn't do it without you. This argument is totally pointless. I'm happy with Aditi and she suits me fine."

"Yeah. I'm sure she suits you perfectly now. All guys look for a woman who they can share their problems with but then the moment they make some money, all they need is a pretty, glamorous airhead to help them spend it," she said bitterly. "Do you think if you weren't rich, a girl like Aditi would even give you a second look?"

"Sheetal, that's just not true," he replied stung. "And that's really insulting. Not just to Aditi but to me too. She's not like that. You've become a mean and bitter person, Sheetal. Maybe

your lawyers can recommend a shrink. I think you need one."
He was very angry at Sheetal for calling Aditi an airhead. Aditi
lived in the moment and enjoyed life. But she was also loving,
loyal and protective of the people she cared about. "And you're
hardly the one to talk about money. You know very well the
house in Atherton is mine. I paid for it. Just because I registered
it in our joint names, it doesn't make it part yours anymore. It
used to be my home."

"It used to be our home, Sanjay. How quickly you've
forgotten everything." She looked away morosely.

"No. You've forgotten, Sheetal. You forgot first, remember.
Don't fight me on this. It'll get really bad really fast," he said
furiously, standing up quickly and almost toppling the chair.
He strode away leaving Sheetal staring at him nervously.

Sanjay tried to control his temper. He exited the hotel and
spotted Aditi in the jewellery shop nearby. He didn't want to
take out his bad mood on Aditi. Especially not after last night.
She was all dressed up today for some weird reason. It had
made him so angry when Sheetal had suggested that Aditi was
not good enough for him, as if Aditi was some dumb bimbo.
And even if she was, it was his choice to go out with whomever
he thought fit. Nobody really had the right to tell him what he
should or shouldn't do any more. It gave him a kick when men
turned around and looked at Aditi and realized that she was
with him. He knew what they were thinking.

"See anything you like?" he asked. "Choose something. I
want to buy you something." He stood behind her and put his
hand around her waist. Her head fit perfectly under his chin
and her hair smelt like vanilla. God knows what she had done
to it, but it fell straight down her back with blonde highlights
now. When he had first met her, it had been wavy and black.

Aditi stomach rumbled. "If I wanted something I would have bought it by now. Aren't you hungry? I just had a sandwich for lunch. I'm starving and Mayank and Jayshree are not back yet."

"Forget about them. They're having a good time. We should too. You've been working so hard today. I thought you said you would have a blast without me," he joked.

"I got bored to go out by myself," she replied.

"You know what? I read a brochure somewhere that the hotel can organize dinner on the beach. Do you want to do that?" he asked enthusiastically.

"There are perfectly good restaurants here," she protested. She wasn't really dressed for the beach.

"Perfectly good isn't perfect. You've been a good girl today. So it's time to have some fun," he said dragging her away. He was like a kid with his favourite toy. And she was his toy, she thought ruefully.

AN UNEXPECTED ENGAGEMENT

"**Y**ou think you can do anything if you flash your credit card around, don't you?" she asked when half an hour later they were sitting at a table for two on the beach. It was very romantic. A waiter was hovering in the background. The table had been set with crisp white linen. Fresh orchids had been arranged in the centre. A bottle of wine was cooling in a bucket nearby. A platter of assorted seafood had been served by a waiter who was standing at a discreet distance where a table had been set up with additional cutlery, drinks and food warmers.

"It's true. There's nothing in the world that can't be arranged with a credit card and an internet connection," he agreed. "And I'm happy I've contributed my bit to this."

"How?" she asked curious.

"My company used to make customized internet banking software. We used to rent out the software to banks. It was fun," he replied.

"If you liked it so much, why did you sell your company?" she asked. It seemed crazy to her to sell something that made you happy.

"I got a very good price for it. That's kind of the whole purpose of creating something, isn't it? You write so that you can sell your books. With software, that becomes even more important. You never know when your technology will become obsolete and your company will become worthless." He paused awkwardly. "And I didn't want to be in touch with Sheetal anymore," he admitted.

"But you'll get bored like this, you know?" she said. "You need to do something constructive again. Nobody can just travel and enjoy life all the time, however great it might sound. A beach resort in Bali is pretty much the same as one in Phuket or Maldives."

"Why are we having this talk about the future? I thought we were doing this fun, no-commitment, living-in-the-moment thing for now. Don't worry. I have Plan B too," he said confidently.

"What is Plan B?" she wanted to know.

He leaned forward and squeezed her hand. "We'll get married," he said, leaning forward and casually popping a shrimp into her mouth. "We'll have five kids. You can write your books. Then I can crib about how you work all the time and never have enough time for me." Aditi was quiet for a long time so he changed the subject. "So what else happened today?"

"Nothing. Just wrote all day," she said quietly.

"Don't worry about me, Aditi. I'm a big boy. I know what I'm doing most of the time. I'm about to sign a contract to develop software for some private hedge funds. There are some other projects that I'm interested in. I'm fine." Sanjay smiled at her.

"What?" she asked, smiling at him nervously. The romantic setting was getting her on edge and she was getting a very serious vibe from him. Hearing about his Plan B hadn't helped. She wondered if he was going to pop out a ring and get down on his knee now. She wasn't ready for that and she didn't want to break up with him either. She wondered what she could do to stop him from proposing to her right now.

"Sanjay, before you say anything there's something I have to tell you," she started off seriously. "I er...can't have any kids." Stupid! Stupid! Stupid! Why did she always say stupid things?

He had just taken a big bite of his fried rice so he just looked at her sympathetically while he chewed. "Is that why you don't want to get married and keep putting it off?" he finally asked when he swallowed. "Look, I don't care about it. We could adopt. Like that couple who adopts kids from around the world. The one with the pouty lips." He waved his fork around his mouth and looked out thoughtfully towards the ocean trying to recollect their names.

"Brad Pitt and Angelina Jolie? How can you not know that?" she asked horrified.

"I can't remember people's names very well," he said grinning. "You don't have to worry about all this anymore. It's my problem too now. I just feel so bad that all this time you've been carrying this burden all by yourself," he told her earnestly.

Aditi gazed at him fondly. He was so sweet. She didn't think she loved anybody more her entire life. He hadn't even bothered to ask what was wrong with her. This was a good thing because she wasn't really sure herself. She must read more about infertility before he began to ask her all the technical details. And he would. He would probably start an extensive internet search as soon as they went back to their room. Sheetal was an idiot to cheat on a guy like him. So what was she doing with him, asked a little voice inside her. She wasn't exactly dying to get married either. She should leave him before it got too serious or he would get hurt again. But she didn't really feel like breaking up with him.

"So?" He prompted.

"So what?" she asked confused.

"Do you want to get married?" he asked anxiously. "What's wrong with you anyway? Isn't there any treatment?"

"It's something to do with the fallopian tubes," she replied vaguely trying to remember some of the things her mother talks about. "Look, you went to so much trouble to set this up. Let's not ruin it with my medical problems."

"Okay," he said reluctantly. "But I want you to know that this doesn't affect the way I feel about you, at all. In fact, it makes me all the more determined to marry you."

Of course he was more determined now, she thought. Sanjay loved a challenge. She was so stupid to have forgotten that. She closed her eyes briefly. It was so ridiculous to lie. "There's nothing wrong with me. I'm perfectly able to have kids." She frowned. "Atleast I think I am. I haven't really put it into practice."

He was very still. "Then why did you say that you couldn't?"

"Panic. Reflex action. Old habits die hard. Take your pick. I thought it would put you off. I couldn't do it." She felt a bit woozy. She didn't know if it was the alcohol or the big decision she had just taken. She wasn't really sure she wanted to get married but she knew she wanted to make Sanjay happy. He deserved to be happy and she wanted to be the one to do it.

"You don't have to lie to me to get out of this," he said seriously. "Just say the words and I won't bother you again."

Aditi thought about that. She wanted him to bother her. It always felt good when he bothered her. She mentally crossed her fingers. Maybe it will work out, she thought to herself. "I guess it could work. The two of us, I mean," she echoed her thoughts aloud.

He broke into an astonished smile. "Not the most enthusiastic response, but I'll take it. So you'll marry me?" he asked with disbelief. Was this all it took? A romantic spot and a little alcohol? Now he knew why other men put so much thought into a proposal. He hoped she wouldn't regret her decision in the morning. He should get it in writing before she could change her mind. He should have bought a ring... nothing like cold, hard diamonds to tilt the odds in your favour.

"Why aren't you on bended knee? And where's my ring?" she demanded as if she had read his mind.

Sanjay ran his hand worriedly in his hair. "You know that I would do anything for you. But don't make me go down on my knees, Aditi. It won't be as pretty as you think it'll be. All this romance stuff is really not my style." He stood up distractedly. "We were just at the jewellery shop. I told you to get something. Why didn't you? Maybe tomorrow..."

"Relax. I was joking," she said pulling him down. Was she really engaged now? She didn't know if she should be happy or horrified. She stared at him speculatively. "So you'll marry me, no matter what?"

Sanjay sensed some mischief ahead. "Yes," he said cautiously.

"Maybe now will be a good time to discuss any abnormal activities that you indulge in that I might want to abstain from," she asked teasingly.

Sanjay's eyes widened. "I don't have any. Do you?"

"I have plenty but I don't want to scare you off. You're sure you can handle me?" She laughed. "Why do you have that clause anyway?"

"I went on a date with this girl once and the next day she took me to this weird swinger's party," he muttered.

"In the US?" asked Aditi fascinated.

"In Hyderabad," he replied.

"Rubbish. Sleepy, old Hyderabad! I don't believe it."

"It's true. I was there. In a farmhouse. I couldn't believe it either. But you don't know what happens to people after a few snorts of coke."

"Coke? You don't do drugs, do you?" she asked, suddenly concerned. "Because that's really not my scene."

"Of course not, Aditi. Don't you know me by now?" He looked at her surprised.

Did she know him? The question bothered her. She had jumped into bed with him. Come to Phuket with him. But did she know him? He never really talked about himself and he didn't have anybody around him except for Mayank. All everybody talked about was how rich and smart he was. The rest of his life was a total question mark. It was like he appeared from nowhere and totally swept her off her feet.

SOMETIMES THINGS GET MESSY

Aditi woke up late the next day. Sanjay had already left for the conference. She felt sluggish. She hadn't slept all night, so she had watched Sanjay sleeping next to her. Is this how she wanted to spend the rest of her life, she wondered. No booming voice from above had enlightened her. God was probably busy with other more important things. Her mundane problems did not concern Him.

She wondered if she had done the right thing by getting engaged. This wasn't how women feel after the man they loved proposed to them, she thought crossly. She should feel ecstatic, but all she could feel was vague sense of unease. She weighed the pros and cons. She took the notepad and pencil from the table next to her and wrote, "Pros" in capitals and underlined it thrice for effect. Her parents and Sanjay would be very happy. That was something. She wrote that down. Her head began to ache from all the thinking. She wrote Aditi Bolisetti and underlined it. It sounded pretty cool. Almost Italian. She was being ridiculous, she told herself sternly and got up. She needed a shower and some food.

Sanjay had left a mess as usual. She put away his used

clothes and picked up some of his papers from the floor. Couldn't he see the dustbin properly, she grumbled and made a face. She put the papers in the dustbin. There's one reason not to get married right here. She couldn't tolerate messy people. She picked up his used towels from the floor and hung them in the bathroom. When the room had been tidied up to her satisfaction, she went for a shower.

After she had changed, she felt much better. She went to the restaurant to have breakfast. Aditi helped herself to some scrambled eggs, hash browns, baked beans, muffins and croissants from the buffet and made her way back to her table. She noticed Sheetal sitting quietly in the corner having breakfast alone and made her way to her.

"Do you mind if I join you? I noticed you're sitting all by yourself." said Aditi with a nervous smile.

"Why? Do you want to rub your relationship with Sanjay in my face?" asked Sheetal morosely.

"No. Of course not. I'm not that kind of a person." She placed her plate down and looked at Sheetal horrified.

"You're going to eat all that. How do you stay so slim?" Sheetal asked enviously.

Aditi smiled and sat down. "I work out. Why aren't you at the conference?"

"Sanjay is speaking today. I don't think he wants me to be there. We had a bit of a fight yesterday." Sheetal ate the last of her toast and gulped down her coffee. "Okay. It was nice meeting you again. I hope you and Sanjay are happy together. He's actually a great guy. Very eager to please," said Sheetal wistfully. She got up to leave.

"Wait," exclaimed Aditi impulsively. "Is that all you're eating? It must have driven Sanjay nuts."

"It did," replied Sheetal amused. They both laughed. "If I ate whatever I wanted, I'll be as big as this hotel."

"Tell me more stuff about Sanjay," demanded Aditi. "Eager to please? Please clarify. I beg you."

Sheetal became thoughtful. "Hmm. I think it's because he doesn't have much family and he doesn't make friends easily. So when he likes somebody he'll do anything for them. You could use that to your advantage, you know."

"As soon as I'm done with my breakfast, I'm taking notes," promised Aditi. "Anything else? He doesn't talk much about himself or his parents."

"Nothing. I'm sure you don't need my perspective about Sanjay. You'll have more fun discovering stuff about him by yourself. You've done a pretty good job till now," said Sheetal laughing. "Tell him I'll give him back his precious house. I don't want his property. It was only because of all the memories, you know. Maybe I need to give it up if I want to move on with my life." Sheetal's eyes became moist. "Look at me. Confiding in you, of all people. Sanjay was right. You are an expert in relationships."

"Not as great in my own relationships as I am at solving other people's problems," confided Aditi ruefully.

"Hi, Ladies. What's going on?" asked Sharad as he slipped into the vacant seat next to Aditi with his orange juice and bowl of cornflakes. "Why so sad? Did you read one of Aditi's novels?" he asked Sheetal, noticing her woebegone face.

"How come you're alone today, Sharad? Where's the rest of your gang?" Aditi asked.

"I'm sick of them. Bunch of drunks. If I have to sit in another tuk-tuk or have another girl ask me if I want a massage, I'm going to lose it," replied Sharad disgruntedly. He looked at Sheetal speculatively.

"Oh. I forgot. This is Sheetal. Sheetal this is Sharad." Aditi said casually.

"Do you have any plans for today, Aditi? We could go see some places or something," said Sharad.

"Sounds good. Do you want to join us Sheetal?" asked Aditi politely.

Sheetal looked at Sharad with interest. "I was thinking of doing some shopping. Not that it ever does me any good. I'm not able to carry off anything like you do, Aditi."

"Oh. Don't worry. You're in expert hands today. Right Sharad?" joked Aditi.

Sharad turned the full force of his smile on Sheetal. "Right," he said good-naturedly. Sheetal looked at Sharad awe-struck.

In the evening, Aditi returned to her room to find Sanjay already in the room. He was frantically searching through all his papers. Aditi put down her packages on the floor and turned to Sanjay concerned. "What's wrong?"

"I had kept some papers on this table yesterday. You haven't seen it by any chance? It was very important." He looked at Aditi anxiously.

Aditi looked around the room. Suddenly she was filled with dread. "Was it something about Veritas Ventures and Tangential?" she asked, feeling sick.

"Yes. Have you seen it?" asked Sanjay hopefully.

Dread turned to fear. "Yes," she said in a small voice. "It was lying on the floor. I put in the dustbin."

"What? Why?" he asked confused.

"I was clearing up your mess. I thought it was trash," she said dully.

"My mess?" said Sanjay, his voice dangerously soft. "Did I ask you to clear up my mess, Aditi? For somebody who was not too keen on getting married, you're acting pretty wifely. Who asked you touch my stuff?"

Aditi felt like he had slapped her. "I wasn't snooping through your stuff. I was just making the room presentable. If you don't want me to behave wifely, maybe we shouldn't get married. I'm not the least bit interested in touching you or your stuff." She turned and walked out of the door, slamming the door behind her. Aditi felt the tears streaming down her face. She was okay to sleep with and have fun with but not good enough to touch his stuff. She wiped them quickly with the back of her hand. She went towards the swimming pool thankful that it was deserted and dark. She sank into a bench and watched the undulating water. She wondered what she was getting into with Sanjay. This was exactly the reason why she didn't want to get married. She couldn't take all this drama.

She didn't know how long she was sitting there in the dark, but she wished she had brought her iPod or her laptop. She was beginning to get bored. The anger had gone out of her. She was so dumb. Sheetal had probably never done anything so stupid when she was with Sanjay, she thought miserably. Why hadn't she checked what she was throwing out? He had every right to be angry. She would be livid too, if he had thrown her things in the trash. She buried her face in her hands. She could never face him again. She wondered if it was possible for her to leave tomorrow. Fresh tears poured down her cheeks. She sensed somebody approaching. She turned to see Sanjay standing a few feet away. She wiped her face on her sleeve.

"I've been searching for you for an hour," he said gruffly. He came and sat next to her on the bench.

She looked at him warily. "I'm sorry for throwing away your papers."

"I'm sorry I told you not to touch my stuff. You can touch anything of mine, anytime you want." He grinned wickedly. She leaned against his arm. "I have something for you." He took out a jewellery box from his pocket. "I don't want you complaining twenty years from now about how I cheated you out of a proper proposal. So…" He got down on one knee as Aditi stared in amazement. "It's a good thing it's so dark here. I couldn't do this in broad daylight," he grumbled. "Aditi Patil, will you marry me?" He took her hand and slipped the ring on her finger. Aditi continued to stare at him. Tears flowed down her face freely. She didn't bother to wipe them away. "Say something. I look like a fool."

"Yes," she said softly. She wrapped her arms around his neck and he stood up with her in his arms. He lost his balance. "Sanjay, no," she yelled as they both fell into the pool.

"I told you it won't be romantic," he gasped after he came up for air. He looked around for Aditi. She was struggling to keep her head above the water.

"Help. Help me. I can't swim," she yelled in a panic as she swallowed the chlorinated water.

"Aditi, it's only four feet of water. Just put your feet down," he instructed.

"Oh," said Aditi, feeling foolish. She stood in the water. "You're wrong. It's the most romantic thing anybody has ever done for me." She stared at him and then launched herself in his arms. He went under again.

PILLOW TALK

"So? What do you taste?" Sanjay asked lazily as he gave a blindfolded Aditi a sip of wine and kissed her.

"You," said Aditi dreamily.

"And now?" He gave her another sip and kissed her again.

"You with a hint of…oh…pepper?" she asked confused.

"Very good. You're learning fast." He kissed her again as a reward. "That's a Californian Zinfandel." He placed the wine glass on the table next to him and collapsed on the bed.

Aditi took off the blindfold and clapped her hands. If this was the punishment she got for throwing away his papers, she should throw some of his stuff away everyday. "Just one more," she begged.

"No more, Aditi. I need a break," pleaded Sanjay.

"You're right. We should get up. Mayank and Jayshree are going to be really pissed that we're ignoring them. I want to see their faces when we tell them we got engaged." She tried to get up.

"I wanted a break from the wine, not from you." He

caught her wrist and pulled her back into the bed. "Mayank and Jayshree won't be angry. I know a lot of stories about them from when they were dating. They'll understand."

Aditi looked at him. He looked cute lying around in just a pair of worn-out old shorts with an unshaven face. She liked him like this. Most of the time, he was always perfectly groomed. He looked formal even when he was wearing jeans. She was going to change all that, she thought, as she snuggled into his arms. She wished she had remembered to buy him some clothes yesterday. She'd had enough of his polo T-shirts. "Do you get a wholesale rate on Ralph Lauren khakis and polo T-shirts or are you personally against all other kinds of clothes?" she asked him picturing him in a white kurta.

He didn't bother to answer. Sometimes Aditi's conversations made no sense to him.

"I forgot to tell you. Sharad, me and Sheetal went shopping yesterday. We managed to get Sheetal some outfits that look great on her. She really doesn't know what suits her at all," Aditi said absent-mindedly. "I should have got some clothes for you too. I totally forgot."

"You, Sharad and Sheetal?" asked Sanjay, raising his eyebrows. "Did I miss something?"

"We had a great time. Anyway, Sheetal said she was giving you the house back. She said she was going to expedite the asset something, something. She just wanted it for sentimental reasons. Why couldn't you let her have it? You did live with her. If you were married you would have to give it to her, no?"

Sanjay leaned back against the pillows with his palms under his head. "But we were not married. And this is not some two-bedroom in Kukatpally, Aditi. This is a five million-dollar house in Atherton, one of the best neighbourhoods in the US. Besides, I paid for it."

"You have a five-million dollar house," she asked shocked. She sat up on the bed. "Why did you need such a big house for just the two of you?"

Sanjay had no answer to that. He shrugged. "I also have apartments in Bombay, London and Manhattan. We could go there anytime you like. Aren't you glad that you're marrying me?" He sighed when she continued to look shocked. "Don't you listen to anything I say? I think I mentioned it. I could have sold you to an Arab sheikh with your permission and you wouldn't have known."

"Sure. Find ways to make some more money," she said sarcastically. She grew dreamy. "It sounds quiet romantic actually. Imagine getting sold off to a tall, dark and handsome sheikh. Then he'll realize how great I am and fall madly in love with me. Maybe I can write a story about that."

Sanjay looked at her like she had lost her mind. "Is that all you think about?" He glowered at her.

She quickly changed the topic. "If you're that rich, why didn't you give Sheetal the house? She gave you five years of her life. She was there when you were struggling. This all sounds so petty and mean. It's not like you at all."

"I gave her five years of my life too and she cheated on me. Can we not talk about this? You're really ruining the mood," he complained. He sat up and tried to explain. "You've always been the one leaving. You have never been the one who got left behind. A lot of people knew us in the software industry. And then she cheats on me with my friend. Everybody knew except me. It was so humiliating. I've worked really hard for my reputation. There wasn't some doting dad holding my hand through everything."

"There wasn't a doting dad, but there was a doting Sheetal, right Sanjay? We're finally getting to the real issue here. This is about your ego. It's not really about the property," she said smugly.

"Are you going to be like this about everything?" he asked, beginning to get annoyed. "Whose side are you on anyway?"

"I just want you to resolve everything with Sheetal before we get married. Just because you don't have a marriage certificate doesn't mean you don't have any responsibility towards her," she said. "I don't know what kind of life you've been living. Legal tussles with an ex-girlfriend, a contract with me. Everything is so complicated with you." She looked down at the tie in her hands before flinging it away. "And I do know about humiliation. I'm the one who broke off an engagement one day before the wedding, remember? People talked about it for months. A guy tells me one day before the wedding that he won't marry me until my father signs away his property. That's humiliation."

"I'd forgotten about that. I'm sorry," he said coming closer and putting his arm around her.

"I don't like this materialistic, ruthless side of you." She shrugged away his arm.

"What do you want me to do?" he asked wearily.

"You're going to discuss this with Sheetal nicely and resolve everything before we get married. She's trying to be nice and you're behaving like a brat. This is not the way to behave."

"I suppose your way is the right way? All the lying and running around? Such a great way to behave," he remarked sarcastically. He regretted it moments later, when Aditi face fell.

"I'm just trying to preserve a person's dignity. It's not lying. People prefer to be lied to than be dumped," she said moodily.

He tried to hug her again. "If I promise to talk to Sheetal will you let this topic drop? This is our last day here. Let's not fight okay?"

"Okay." She smiled as his hand started wandering around her body. The man was insatiable. "I thought you were done," she grumbled. She had a bright idea. "You think you can pretend to be an Arab sheikh who just bought me?"

He looked pained. "Oh God…why? Can't we just be normal for a change?"

She looked insulted. "Normal is boring. Somebody told you I was normal? Who?"

He gave up. He pulled her into his arms and kissed her. "Okay. What does an Arab sheikh do?"

"Don't get so excited," she informed him demurely. "I'm just doing research for my story."

Later in the afternoon, Aditi woke up and pushed Sanjay awake. She had never behaved in such a crazy way before. "I'm going down. People are going to think we died. You can stay here if you want." She disappeared into the bathroom and emerged a few minutes later.

"Sorry. I'm being rude. I don't usually get an opportunity to behave like this. It's addictive. You're addictive," he said with a wicked grin.

"Can I ask you something personal?" Aditi asked when she was fully dressed.

He looked at her questioningly. "Isn't it a bit late to be formal?" he said, getting up.

"Do you ever think that maybe you came back to India for some other reason and not just to get married?" she asked him thoughtfully.

"Oh God! More deep questions that I don't want to think about," he groaned. "Aditi, you're being such a bore. Why are you thinking about all this today?" He pulled her towards him. "Make me forget now," he ordered, pulling her hips towards his and resting his forehead against hers.

"What's got into you?" she said laughing. She pushed him towards the bathroom. "Go!"

He went into the bathroom, but her words still rankled. Did there have to be a reason behind everything he did? He hated it when Aditi tried to analyze him.

They went downstairs in search of the rest. They found Jayshree, Mayank, Sheetal and Sharad in the coffee shop.

"So you both finally decided to get up," said Jayshree.

"What did you guys do today?" Aditi asked Sheetal taking the seat next to her. "Did you go out with Sharad?" she asked Sheetal excitedly.

"We went out for lunch. It was nice. But where's the future, Aditi? He lives in Hyderabad and I live in California." Sheetal played with the long strand of beads around her neck that Aditi had chosen for her yesterday.

Don't worry. If you both really like each other, you'll find a way," said Aditi soothingly.

"Look at that," said Mayank to Sanjay. "Your ex-girlfriend and your current girlfriend are best friends. How nice for you!"

"I don't care. I have nothing to hide," said Sanjay defensively. "And by the way, Aditi and I are engaged now."

"Great." "When did this happen?" came the responses, almost in unison. Jayshree and Sheetal leaned over to admire Aditi's ring. It was a beautiful two-carat solitaire with tiny diamonds arranged around it.

"Have you told your parents?" asked Jayshree. "What do you think they'll say?" She loved the way Aditi just took decisions without worrying about anybody's opinion. She always wished she could be like that.

"Do you really need to ask? They'll be ecstatic," replied Aditi. "It's the moment they have waiting for all their life."

"It's been an eventful few days, hasn't it? I don't feel like going back tomorrow," murmured Jayshree as she leaned on Mayank's arm.

"We should celebrate. Let go to that famous place tonight. What's its name? 7th floor? 6th floor?" asked Mayank.

"The 9th floor," replied Sheetal. She turned to Sanjay enthusiastically. "It's really good. Great Mediterranean food. Remember when we went to Europe. Exactly like that."

"Yeah," said Sanjay, looking awkwardly at Aditi. But Aditi just beamed at them. "It's so nice that you guys are getting along," she said hugging Sanjay. "Isn't this so much better?"

Sanjay just rolled his eyes. "It's great. Just one big happy family." He turned to Sheetal. "Umm... Aditi told me you'll transfer the house to me. Thanks. You can keep all the other stuff. I just want my house back, okay? Can I tell Naveen?"

"Sure. Thanks." Sheetal smiled awkwardly at him. Sharad was listening carefully to the conversation. "You're very quiet," Sheetal whispered to Sharad.

"You're going back tomorrow. I think I'll miss you," he said softly.

Sanjay looked at the two of them. Sheetal and Sharad? There was something a little incestuous about that. Maybe there was something in the water around here. Or the air of casual sexiness that Phuket seemed to exude. But Sheetal wasn't his problem anymore. Tomorrow they were all going back to their normal lives and he hoped Aditi wouldn't change her mind about getting married when reality came knocking.

LOVE ME FOR WHAT I AM

Aditi honked at the car in front of her and rushed through the amber light before it could turn red. Sanjay placed his hand on the dashboard and closed his eyes. Aditi had offered to pick him up because his car was being serviced and he had impulsively agreed. He bitterly regretted it now.

"Can you please let me drive," he implored for the umpteenth time. "I'll let you drive my car if you let me drive yours." He wasn't really eager to drive Aditi's i10 or allow her to drive his Beemer, but he wanted both of them to live at least another twenty years. Aditi took a left turn without slowing down. The pedestrians crossing the road rushed to the other side to avoid being hit. Sanjay gritted his teeth. "There's no emergency. I just want to reach in one piece," he said mildly. He turned on the stereo to take his mind off her driving and played the song 'Kabhi Kabhi Aditi'. It had become his favourite Hindi song lately and it drove Aditi nuts. She changed the song.

"I'm really attached to my car. It's almost my second home. Nobody drives my car," she said as she overtook an RTC bus from the left. He looked around her car. It was obviously her second home. There were two plastic bags on the back seat with some jeans, gym clothes and dresses. Two pairs of high-heeled shoes and sports shoes were tucked under the seat. Her laptop bag and a folder full of printed sheets were lying next to a tennis racquet. There was another tote with cokes, packets of chips and some apples.

Aditi's brows were knitted in concentration. She was wearing a simple cotton sari with long, dangly silver earrings, lots of silver bangles and a bindi. The sari was his idea but the jewellery was her addition. He enjoyed the way she changed her style of dressing according to the situation. She was completely at ease in whatever she wore. Even in those clothes that he had secretly dubbed her hooker outfits. She looked almost like a wife today, he thought sentimentally. Except for the sandals with the nasty-looking heels that she had kicked off to make driving easier. She could easily stab him with those heels.

Aditi could sense his eyes on her. He had looked a bit dumb-struck ever since he had seen her in a sari. She knew exactly what he was thinking. Indian men and their stupid, Yash Chopra-style sari fantasies. "So where are we going? And why do I have to wear a sari," she asked as she deftly swerved to avoid banging into an auto.

"Just watch," he said confidently. But he was a bit nervous inside. He was taking Aditi to see his aunt and show her the house where he grew up. He had never revealed much to Aditi about his parents or his childhood. She had only seen that part of him that had come after his success. Now he knew the time had come to show her his middle-class roots. He hoped she would love that part of him too. He fervently wished Aditi would like his aunt. She was the only relative that he was close to. He hadn't told her they were going to meet his aunt because he didn't want to freak her out and give her a chance to make excuses.

He directed her through the narrow lanes till they reached a modest two-storey house in a middle-class locality. The yellow paint had faded to a dull cream, but the compound was spic and span and clay pots filled with crotons lined the compound wall from inside. There were no landscaped gardens and hardly any space between two houses. Some houses even had a common wall. Aditi shot him a puzzled look and got out of the car.

"Is this your aunt's house?" she asked uncertainly. He shot her a surprised look and nodded. Panic crept into her eyes. "Why didn't you tell me? Does she know we're coming?"

"Yes. She's cool. You don't have to worry. It's not like we need her approval or anything. Just be yourself," he said and held her hand.

"Umm...actually Sanjay. I don't think I can do this today. I had to meet Shree. She asked me to go to the doctor with her today," she said making her way back to the car.

He laughed. "Nice try. That's not going to work anymore." He held her hand till they reached the entrance of the house and he pressed the door-bell. The door was opened by a matronly, middle-aged woman. Sanjay took off his shoes and touched her feet, so Aditi did the same. The woman smiled and said something in Telugu that Aditi couldn't understand. Sanjay laughed.

"I told him that you're very beautiful and I didn't realize that his standards were so high. Now I know why he didn't like any of the girls that I selected for him," said Sanjay's aunt with a smile. "Come sit down."

Aditi sat down on the small sofa. Sanjay sat next to her. Sanjay's uncle came and joined them in the small living room. Sanjay and Aditi got up and touched his feet too.

"My son is also in America. He hasn't come back yet like Sanjay. My daughter lives in the next lane," said Sanjay's uncle cheerfully.

"Attamma and Mamaiya brought me up. I used to live on the main road. It's empty now." Sanjay told her. He wondered what Aditi thought about his aunt's small, two-bedroom house. She was smiling and talking politely to his aunt and uncle, but her face gave nothing away. When he was a kid he used to sleep on a diwan in this very same hall, while his father drank himself into a stupor at night in the next lane.

When his aunt went inside the kitchen to prepare some snacks, Aditi stood up to help. She didn't know what she was going to do in the kitchen, but it seemed like the appropriate thing to do. She was touched that Sanjay trusted her enough to introduce her to his family.

Sanjay's aunt put a *kadai* with oil on one burner of her stove top and heated the chicken curry on another. "We're so happy that Sanjay brought you to meet us. He doesn't come here very often. Mostly we only go and stay with him for a few days whenever we get bored. Now you're there, he'll be okay."

"I don't know about that. Sanjay is very good at taking care of himself. I'm not very good at domestic matters," Aditi said shakily.

"But he has someone now. His mother died of cancer, you know? His father was totally wiped out after that. Financially and emotionally. He was a professor at Osmania. Drank himself to death, useless fellow. Died of liver failure," said Sanjay's aunt bitterly. "He used to be a very quiet boy. He used to sleep and study in the hall outside. Nobody could make out there was a child in the house." Sanjay's aunt began to roll out the puris. "Why don't you take those plates from there and take them outside." She said as she tested if the oil was hot with a tiny ball of dough.

Aditi wordlessly took the plates and went outside. Sanjay looked at Aditi setting the table and wondered what his aunt had told Aditi about him. Her face was thoughtful and a bit downcast. She went inside again and returned with a plate full of puris. When the table was set they all sat down to eat.

"Hmm... this is so good," said Aditi tasting the *aloo bonda* Sanjay's aunt had made. "The ones you get outside aren't so tasty." She tried some *ragi sankati* with the chicken curry. "This is fabulous. I haven't had this before. Tomorrow I'll have to do an hour on the treadmill," she groaned.

"You're so thin, why you have to worry about anything? When you become our age then you can worry about what to eat," said Uncle genially. Aditi chatted pleasantly with Sanjay's aunt and uncle throughout till it was time to leave. Sanjay was subdued. When they were leaving Sanjay's aunt hugged her and made her promise that she would visit again.

When they drove past the next lane, Sanjay pointed to an old house with peeling paint on the main road. "I used to live there when I was a kid. That's my house," he said casually.

"Don't you want to go inside and check if everything is okay?" asked Aditi surprised.

He shrugged. "It's on sale. I don't really care. I haven't lived there for ages."

"The visit with your aunt went well," she commented.

"It went very well," he agreed, running his hand through her hair and caressing her cheek. His hand tried to slip inside her pallu. It was pinned shut. "You were a model fiancee." He tried from another side. That was pinned shut too. "What the hell? Is this how it's supposed to be?" he asked confused. He counted the number of pins on her sari. Four.

She stopped his hand from getting too adventurous. "Did you think you could just unravel my sari like Duryodhana did to Draupadi?" she asked.

"It was Dushasana, not Duryodhana. And never like that, Adi. More like...er...unwrapping my favourite present," he said smiling.

"Well, at least you're smiling. You were looking pretty down back then," she said.

He shook his head. "It's nothing. I love to meet my aunt and uncle but coming here depresses me a bit. I feel like going and getting stinking drunk. Let's do that. Let's go to the *Marriott*."

"I don't think so," she said sternly. "Your aunt put your drinking into a whole new perspective for me," she said concentrating on her driving. She could feel tears pricking eyes. She imagined him as a child. He must have sat in the corner of the house looking out of the window watching other children eat ice-cream with their parents. The tears rolled down faster. She tried to wipe them with her hands.

Sanjay swore. "Pull over," he told her. She slowly changed lanes to come to the left. She stopped the car near the pavement and rested her hands on the steering wheel and burst into tears.

"How your parents let you drive is a mystery to me," he said. "Adi, why are you crying now? Didn't you like my aunt? Did she say something to you?"

"I'm so sorry you couldn't have ice-cream like the rest of the kids," she said in between sobs.

He pulled her into his arms. "I have no idea what you're talking about," he said frustrated. "And we're making a hell of a scene." Traffic was heavy. They were getting curious glances from the passengers of the slow-moving vehicles.

"Your aunt said you were lonely and quiet when you were a kid," she said trying to compose herself.

"Ah! She told you about my father," he said. "I was wondering what she was telling you in the kitchen. Put two women together and all the family skeletons come tumbling out. What has that got to do with ice-cream?"

"I was imagining you as a tiny kid without a mother and not getting any ice-cream," she sniffed.

"Well, for one thing I was thirteen years old and almost six-feet tall when my mother passed away. And even though my father was a bit of an alcoholic, he was a perfectly normal parent. The only reason I used to spend so much time in my aunt's house was because I used to study there and my father had to go to work. He taught Maths in Osmania and then coached some Intermediate kids in the evenings. It wasn't as bad as whatever you're thinking in that overactive head of yours."

"It's still sad," she said feeling a bit better.

"Yeah. Well, everybody has some tragedy in their life. You get used to it," he said. "I could really use a drink now."

"And I'm going to watch your drinking like a hawk," she said glaring at him.

"I'm not like my father. I know when to stop," he protested.

"That's what they all say," she replied unconvinced. He sometimes drank a bit too much. "Let's go home."

"Can I drive now?" He tried again.

"No," she said and started the car, still sniffling.

LOVE MAKES A WOMAN NAG

Sanjay stole a glance at Aditi wondering if she was still emotional. She looked serious. He would cut down on his drinking if it really upset her so much. They passed by his father's coaching centre. "See that building there that says, *Ramana's Techno School.* My dad used to teach there in the evenings. I can't believe it's still open. The building looks like it's falling apart," said Sanjay reminiscing.

Aditi stopped the car in the middle of the road. The car behind them honked rudely. "Your dad taught there? Don't you want to go inside and see it? Maybe somebody you know is still there."

"Adi, You can't stop in the middle of the road," he scolded. The woman was going to drive him to an early grave and she won't let him drink. "Why would I go there?"

"I don't know. You'll know when you go there," said Aditi watching him control his irritation. She tried distraction. "Why is it called a techno school? Is it very high-tech?"

He smiled. "No. Everything just sounds better with a 'tech' attached before or after it."

Aditi parked the car and got out. Sanjay followed. There was no point stopping Aditi once she had made up her mind about something. They climbed the concrete steps and entered the institute. The receptionist looked at them askance. Sanjay looked at Aditi in a panic. "What am I supposed to say?"

"Can we meet the principal or manager? Who is in charge?" asked Aditi. Sanjay looked at the cracked, *paan*-stained walls and dirty windows. He didn't remember it being so bad when his father used to teach here.

"Where is your child? He will have to sit for an entrance before getting admission. Which standard is he in? The admission office is there." She pointed towards another cubicle and eyed them suspiciously.

"We don't want admission. We want to meet the manager. This man's father used to teach here fifteen years ago. His name was..." She looked at Sanjay, but he wasn't following her. He still looked dazed and not in a pleasant way. She elbowed him. "What's your dad's name?"

"Venkatramana Bolisetti," he replied. The receptionist looked at them blankly. "Speak to Prasad Sir. He'll be in that office. Let me ask him if he is free." She picked up the phone and spoke rapidly in Telugu.

"Since when do you have to sit for an entrance test to get into an institute like this," said Aditi disbelievingly.

"You can go inside," said the receptionist looking at them speculatively.

They opened the door that she had indicated. A thin, bespectacled man looked up at them with curiosity. "You're Ramana's son? Sanjay?" he asked.

Sanjay nodded. "Yes Sir."

"What can I do for you?" he asked kindly.

"I was just passing this area. I was wondering if you knew my father," asked Sanjay. This was so ridiculous, he thought. He felt as if he was searching for his long-lost father. His father was dead and he was so over it. If only Aditi would let him be in peace. He sometimes wished Aditi was shallow and superficial. Shallow and superficial women were so easy to please.

"Of course I knew your father. I know you too. All our students know you. Your father used to talk about you all the time. We're all very proud of you too. We keep motivating all our students to study by telling them your story. There's a photo of you on our notice board. Didn't you see it?" The professor's eyes twinkled behind his glasses.

"No," said Sanjay amused.

The old professor and Sanjay stared at each other. "Is there something that I can help you with?" asked Prasad Sir.

"No. I was just passing by and thought I would drop in," said Sanjay awkwardly. He never should have come here. He had nothing in common with these people anymore and he looked foolish. He looked at Aditi. She was beaming at the old man like he was an old friend.

"Do you want to meet our students? Maybe you can give them a talk about how they can achieve their goals," said Prasad Sir in a burst of inspiration. "These kids are so good but they need someone to guide them. I'm going to retire in a few months. My son wants me to move to Australia to live with him. Without somebody to teach and manage, this place will close. There's not much money in this, you know. These children are doing Intermediate privately and they don't have money for coaching. Some of them even work in shops and restaurants in the daytime to support their families. They don't even have time to study. When people like you achieve something and come back to their country to make things better, there's hope for the next generation. If someone like you could spare some time…"

Sanjay suddenly began to feel claustrophobic. He stood up. "I'm a little busy right now and I have to go to the US next week. I'm starting a new business. Let me think about it. I'll check my schedule and get in touch with you. Meanwhile, if you need any money to purchase any equipment or furniture or anything. I can help with that."

"Of course. Of course. You're a busy man. I understand. Whatever help you can give is always welcome." Prasad Sir smiled genially. "I hope I haven't offended you."

"Oh no. No Sir," said Sanjay scribbling his phone number and email address on a piece of paper and handing it to Prasad Sir. "I'll be in touch. This is my phone number. I don't have a business card right now." He took the card that Prasad Sir handed to him and shook his hand.

When they were leaving the institute, Aditi went up to the notice board to check out Sanjay's photo. A young boy with a thin face and budding mustache looked back at her earnestly from an old newspaper clipping. "You topped the state in the tenth and the twelfth? Why am not surprised? Is that how you used to look? That's so cute. You used to wear glasses. Where are they?" She burst out laughing.

"Lasik," he said embarrassed. "I was in the tenth in this picture and I wasn't even remotely cute."

"You've come a long way," she said softly.

"A long, long way," he agreed. "And I'm not sure I want to go back, Adi."

"Who's telling you to go back? He's asking you to help these kids get ahead. What you want to do is entirely upto you, of course," she reminded him. They made their way back to the car.

"Why does everybody expect so much from me? Why do you care about what I do?" he muttered.

"I don't care what you do as long as you're happy. It's just that, sometimes when we're in a group, you're always a little bit aloof from all of us. When we crib about our parents, you don't say anything about yours. I thought maybe if you made peace with your past or something. I don't know. In the end it's up to you. Whatever works." She shrugged and started the car.

Sanjay was quiet for a long time. Craig David's 'Rise and fall' about a superstar who had forgotten his roots played in an endless loop. He was about to comment about it when understanding dawned on him. "That's really not fair, Aditi. I'm not like that at all. I haven't forgotten my values. I have changed certain aspects of my life that weren't working before. I'm not hurting anybody. If I want to live my life the way that suits me, it's not wrong."

"I was wondering when you'll catch on," she exclaimed. She changed the song. Travie McCoy's 'Billionaire' came on. Sanjay glared at her. He punched the buttons on her stereo furiously. "You're going to break it today," she said laughing. "You're obviously avoiding something. Attamma, says you've come out here just twice in the past six months. They pretty much raised you and yet you're not comfortable visiting them. It's not natural."

Sanjay felt silent again. He stared out of the window. Aditi wondered if she had said too much. She was about to speak when he turned back to her. "Let me explain something to you. When I first became successful, I was doing whatever I could for everybody. But people take advantage of that. You become the first person that everyone goes to when they need a loan or a job or a reference. After a while, that's all they need you for… to do stuff for them. I'm not responsible for everybody's life. I have my own crap to deal with."

"I'm not telling you to help people if you don't want to but there's a reason you came to Hyderabad. You keep saying that you came to India to get married. I don't believe that. I'm sure there were plenty of girls in the US who you could marry, but you didn't. Think about it. Why did you come back here? Why not London? Or Bombay? Or New York? You have houses there, don't you? What's here for you?"

Sanjay thought about that. Why had he chosen Hyderabad? He stared out of the window without seeing anything in particular. He knew this road well and could probably drive on this road in his sleep. There was something comforting about that. Sometimes coming back to your hometown felt like coming back to family, even though there was not much of a family left. "Okay. I'll see what I can do. Maybe I can find somebody to manage the place. I don't know. I don't need this extra work. Why don't you do it?" he asked.

"You're not going to make this my responsibility. I'm pretty busy already," said Aditi.

"With what?" he asked laconically. "Shopping and going out?"

Aditi gave him a dirty look. "Actually, I have my own website and it takes a lot of my time. I also do a lot of counselling work for *Sahaas*. I don't want to brag now, but I do a lot of charity work. That's not the point. This is something you have to do, not me. You never talk about your relatives or your childhood or your parents. There's something you need to work out. I think you know it and that's why you came back," she said when he continued to look at her. "You know, we don't know a lot about each other. And you never talk about yourself. I didn't even know your dad's name. Are we doing the right thing by getting engaged so soon?"

"Are you having doubts about me?" Sanjay asked softly. He had thought things were going great.

Aditi felt ashamed. He looked confused and troubled. She didn't know why she was pestering him about stuff that he wasn't comfortable with but she couldn't let it go. "No. Sometimes. Marriage is a big step. It's about combining our families, our pasts and our futures. It's not just about opening joint accounts and setting up a house. I don't know how to make you understand." She changed lanes and the Toyota behind them honked.

Sanjay closed his eyes. "Can't you stick to one lane?" he grumbled. He cautiously opened one eye, then the other. "You don't have to be nervous. If you're having doubts just tell me. We don't have to rush into anything." He gaze dropped to the ring on her finger and up again at her face.

Aditi twisted the ring around her finger nervously with her thumb. "I can't," she murmured. "I like my ring too much." They both laughed.

"Then keep it. Think of it as a gift." He smiled crookedly. "It's not like I can wear it."

She was thoughtful for a while. Marriage scared her but

Sanjay wanted to get married and she loved him and wanted to be with him. It was a no-brainer really. "It's an engagement ring and that's how it's going to be," she said finally.

Sanjay was relieved to hear her answer and to have a change of topic. If he had issues, he didn't want to think about them right now. "Want to have some *biryani*? You get great stuff here," he said pointing to the board of *Paradise Restaurant*.

"Sanjay, we just ate," groaned Aditi.

He cleared his throat. "Umm…my parents used to get me here when I was a kid every Sunday afternoon."

Aditi fingers tightened momentarily on the wheel. She reached out and squeezed his arm. "Maybe we should get some then," she said softly.

GETTING TO KNOW YOU BETTER

Aditi and Sanjay were in *Home and Living* looking for a sofa set for Sanjay's living room. She liked the overstuffed suede couches in olive while Sanjay was leaning towards the sleek black leather ones. Every sofa that he liked was in black leather. He had an obsession with it. She wondered what he would think of her black leather jeans. She should wear them sometime just to see his reaction. Or better yet she should order one of those black leather bustiers from *Agent Provocateur*... with a whip. Maybe he was into that stuff. She smiled to herself.

"What's so funny?" Sanjay asked her. He was sitting on his favourite black couch with his arms across his chest prepared for battle. Like a five-year old who wanted his favourite toy and wouldn't leave the toy store without it.

"Nothing. You should get the black leather one if you like it so much. After all, it's your house," she told him drily.

"No. No. I want you to like it too," he said. "It's going to be your house too when we get married. You have to like everything too." He came and stood in front of her and looked at her earnestly. "I even told Naveen that I don't want a prenup. If we don't work out, having all this stuff won't matter anyway." He smiled his quirky, crooked smile.

A lump formed in her throat. This was really huge for Sanjay. Even though he kept claiming he wanted to get married, he hadn't really given her any indication that he trusted her till today. For him to trust her in this way was more touching than his marriage proposal. What had he said when they had first started going out? Something about loving her with pimples and during illness and growing old together. She suddenly realized what that meant.

"I like the black one too. They're okay," she said blinking back tears.

"No. I'm fine with the green ones," he said hastily, noticing her tears. She seemed quite overwhelmed about the sofas. He wondered if buying furniture was an emotional experience for her. She had said that she liked decorating. It would be interesting to see how she behaved when she hated something.

"Olive. They're olive," she said, sniffling into a tissue.

"Whatever," he said looking at her strangely. "Shall I tell the sales guy we're taking this one?"

Aditi was too overwhelmed with her feelings to say anything. Why was she acting like an idiot? She shook her head. "Black. We'll take the black one."

"You're sure about this?" he asked concerned. She just nodded.

They were making their way to the payment counter when Aditi saw Nikhil and his wife in the linen section. He was looking at some table mats with his wife. Aditi looked at Sanjay to see if he had noticed them. When she looked back at them, she realized, to her horror, that they too were making their way to the payment counter. She grabbed Sanjay's hand.

"Wait. There's something else I wanted to see," she said panicked and dragged a startled Sanjay away from the counter. She searched for a place to hide. The only place that she could find was the toilet. She pulled him inside the toilet and heaved a sigh of relief.

"You wanted to see the toilet?" he asked confused. It was going to take forever to understand Aditi.

"I wanted to try making out in a public place. I saw it in a movie once," she said putting her arms around his neck.

"But this toilet's really dirty," he said surprised.

"Jayshree swears by it," she said absent-mindedly running her hands under his shirt. She wondered if Nikhil had left.

"Jayshree and Mayank?" he asked incredulously. He did not want to picture it. He forced his mind to go blank. "She told you that?" He winced when he thought about what highly-intimate, juicy detail Aditi had revealed about him to get that gem out of Jayshree. Stupid girl talk.

"She highly recommends it. They did it on the beach in Phuket and in KBR Park and she's totally hooked," she replied kissing him. "You know what? You're right. It won't work. Let's go." Nikhil would have left by now. It was safe for them to go out.

Sanjay held her tighter. "We could try, if you really want to." Aditi constantly surprised him. He wondered if he would ever get enough of her. He didn't think he could ever look at Mayank with a straight face though.

"You just said it was filthy. Let's go," she said quickly, dragging an even more confused Sanjay back out.

As they were making their way back to the payment counter, Sanjay saw a familiar couple at the exit. Recognition flooded through him. "You were running away from him again, weren't you?" His jaw tightened with irritation. He grabbed Aditi's hand and pulled her towards them. "I'm going to settle this once and for all with this dickhead."

"No. We can't. Please Sanjay. Don't." She stared at him with horror. He stared back in frustration.

"Why not?" He shot back.

"They have kids," whispered Aditi. "And the sales guy is waiting for us and you're creating a scene."

He looked at the salesman and a few other customers looking at him with puzzlement and made his way to the counter reluctantly. "Okay. But this is the last time you're hiding from them. Promise?" Aditi nodded. Some people where still looking at them curiously.

He didn't know what was wrong with him. Was he actually thinking of picking up a fight with Aditi's ex in a huge department store? It was so unlike him. It was as if his brain went to sleep whenever he was with Aditi. Especially if one of her ex-boyfriends was in the vicinity.

When they reached home after their furniture shopping, Sanjay's maid, Lakshmi, was in the kitchen washing the dishes. She eyed them suspiciously and updated Sanjay on the latest buzz going around the colony. She said something to him snidely in Telugu looking pointedly at Aditi. Sanjay smiled and bantered with her for a bit till his phone buzzed. He excused himself to answer the call.

Aditi went into the dining area to admire their newly purchased dining table. She pulled out a chair and sat down, running her hand over the polished teak. A huge asymmetrical platter in green glass adorned the centre. She had bought it in Indonesia two years ago and it looked fabulous on the table. Correction! It would look fabulous if Sanjay hadn't dumped a handful of USB drives and batteries in it. The man obviously had no sense. She was just about to lecture him about clutter management when he sat beside her and dropped his phone into the bowl.

"That bowl is not for your odds and ends," she said annoyed.

"Then what's it for?" he asked.

"Nothing. It just looks good on the table," she replied.

"Everything in life should have a purpose besides just looking good," he said frowning.

"Well. Ok then. Put some fruit in it," she said exasperated.

"Then where will I put my USBs?" he wanted to know.

"How about your office?" she asked the logical question.

"Why would I keep them in my office?" he asked puzzled. "I use my laptop on the dining table. I eat in my office."

Breathe. Breathe. Count to ten. Relationships were about compromise. Didn't she decide that she was going to make it work with Sanjay? After all he had compromised about the dining table. He had wanted the chrome and glass one. So she had compromised on the sofas. Okay she hadn't technically compromised on the sofas. He had just caught her at a weak moment. She still thought they were hideous. But they were learning to compromise. What's a little mess in the path of true love?

She changed the subject. "What was Lakshmi saying about me?"

"She said that I shouldn't dilly-dally and that we should get married soon. My neighbours are beginning to talk about us," he replied.

"What are they saying about us?" she asked curious.

"They are confused about the state of our relationship. They don't know if they should befriend you or gossip about you."

"What did you tell her?" she asked interested.

"I told her she should concentrate on doing her work properly and not engage in idle gossip," he said grinning. "So what do you want to do for dinner? Do you want to go out or order in?"

"Let's eat at home. I'm going to cook dinner," she said generously.

"You can cook?" he asked doubtfully. He had never even seen her making tea.

"Well, I haven't really done it before, but how hard could it be?" she said confidently.

"A kitchen virgin," he muttered. "This should be entertaining."

Aditi went into the kitchen and put a pan on the stove. She turned on the stove and looked around. Sanjay leaned against the wall and watched her. Lakshmi stopped wiping the counter and looked at her. She turned around and spoke to Sanjay in rapid Telugu.

"What are you cooking? Air?" he asked amused.

"Oh right. I knew that. What do you have that can be cooked?" she said opening cupboards. Lakshmi laughed and spoke to Sanjay again. Sanjay replied. They both laughed heartily.

"Ok. What is your maid saying about me?" she said annoyed.

"She saying that it's a good thing that I got to know that you can't cook before I married you,"

"And what did you tell her?" she asked.

"I said it was okay," he said with a straight face.

"It sounded like you said a lot more than that," she muttered.

They finally prepared a simple dinner of *rotis* and *bhendi*. Sanjay patiently explained the exact chemistry and physics behind making perfectly soft *rotis* and crisp *bhendi* when he saw her papad-like *rotis* and slimy *bhendi*. At least she had managed to make his maid happy. She was still laughing merrily when it was time for her to leave. After dinner, when she had got out her laptop to work on her blog, he hadn't protested. He had simply brought out his own.

Aditi looked up from her laptop to watch Sanjay following the US markets on his laptop. They had spent the last hour sitting on his landscaped balcony in total silence. She liked that about him. He could shut up when she wanted him to shut up.

Sanjay looked up from his laptop and their eyes met. She smiled. "What are you doing so seriously?" he asked.

"Just writing this blog I do. It's getting quite popular," she said happily. Today had been a perfect day even though they hadn't done anything exciting and they had bumped into Nikhil at the store.

"Really? Send me the link. I want to read it," he said. He opened her mail and looked at her in surprise. "You're Ms Loveleen? I should have known...all the mushy advice. Why didn't you tell me before? I love her blogs. I mean your blogs. I write to her all the time."

"You read my blog? You don't look like somebody who would read a relationship blog," said Aditi pleasantly surprised.

"There was a time in my life that I was very confused. I needed all the help I could get," he said wryly. "I think your blog is fabulous." He put his laptop aside. "You know what you should do? You should go through all your best articles and put it together as a book. Like a relationship, self-help book. Find out all the publishers who publish non-fiction and ask them if they are interested. I'm sure that there'll be a few who are. I mean Ms Loveleen is huge. A lot of people I know follow it. People who follow your blog will automatically read your book. You can even monetize your blog. Didn't you know?"

"Monetize it?" asked Aditi confused. "I don't want to make money from the site. I want to help people. I like reading what people have to say. People will stop visiting the site if I charge them."

"You don't charge people. You put ads on your website. Let me show you. What's your password?" He picked up his laptop and loaded her page. He made some adjustments to her page. "Now, everytime somebody loads your page, you'll get paid. There are other things you can do. Give me a few days to figure it out."

"You know, you may be on to something," she said, getting excited. "I love to write about relationships. Why didn't I think about this before?"

"Because you don't have my great mind," he said standing up. "You need to thank me properly for my idea." He pulled her towards the bedroom. "So, I'm going to be this arrogant, powerful publisher and you can be the struggling writer who tries to get her book published by offering her lovely body to the publisher."

"Why am I always doing the begging?" she protested.

"Because you look so pretty when you do it," he told her firmly.

FACING RESPONSIBILITIES

Sanjay looked around the half done Tangential office and was happy with the progress the interior designer had made. He wished he had had the foresight to hire an interior designer to do up his house instead of trying to do it himself. He would have saved himself a lot of trouble. It was a good thing that Aditi had stepped in at the right time or he would still be sleeping on the floor with the sawdust covering him.

His father's house flashed before his eyes. He cursed Aditi for making him remember things that he had happily forgotten. He had already decided that he was going to sell the house. Aditi was not going to make him feel guilty about letting go of things that he had every right to forget. On the other hand, it was a good piece of real estate in the heart of Koti. It would appreciate even if he held on to it, he thought.

"Hey Vinay. There's another house I own that I want to redo. Do you have the time right now? I want to show it you."

An hour later, Sanjay and Vinay were standing in the middle of Sanjay's childhood home. "What do you want done to it?" asked Vinay when he had finished checking the basic structure of the house.

Sanjay was stumped. "Er…maybe you could knock down a couple of walls and convert it into some classrooms and labs," he was surprised to hear himself say. "Maybe build a couple of floors. I don't think you should have too much trouble with building permissions."

Vinay agreed. "It'll be within the permissible limit. You want to open a school here?" asked Vinay suprised.

"Not a school. Just an institute." Sanjay checked the doors and windows. "The basic structure seems fine."

Vinay agreed. "It's solid. They don't build houses like these anymore. I'll draw up the plans and show it to you by next week."

On his way back to the office, Sanjay passed by the institute. He slowed down and looked up at the crumbling building. He sat in the car wondering if he actually had the energy to do what he was about to do. He got out of the car and slowly walked towards the centre.

When he entered, no one asked him who he was. The receptionist immediately sent him into Prasad Sir's office. Prasad Sir greeted him with a warm smile. "You're back from you trip? We were wondering if we would ever see you again," he said candidly.

"I always keep my promises," replied Sanjay slightly embarassed. He didn't want to confess about how close he had been from backing out.

Prasad Sir got up and escorted Sanjay to the classroom. Twenty pairs of eyes stared at Sanjay curiously. "Your father was a great man. He tutored so many poor children for very little money. If he was alive he would very proud of you," said the professor beaming.

Sanjay felt the familiar heaviness settle in his chest whenever he thought about his father. It suprised him that he could still feel so emotional about his growing up years. His father had found time for a lot of things but he hadn't had time to look after him, he thought, the bile rising in his throat. He tried to get the thought out of his mind but it persisted like a particularly virulent strain of bacteria. It took all his self control to get his attention back to the students.

"What exactly do you want me to do?" he asked Prasad Sir carefully.

"I have been thinking of retiring. I need somebody to take over. If you could find somebody to takeover or take charge yourself..." The professor stopped when he saw the terrified expression on Sanjay's face. "Or you could just teach. Whatever you're comfortable with. It was started by your father," Prasad Sir reminded him gently. "The rent is very low so they don't bother repairing anything. If this place closes the students will be alone again. They can't afford extra tutions..." The professor trailed off again.

Sanjay was quiet for a while. He always knew it would come to this. Why else would he have told Vinay to do up his old house before he had even come here? He was slowly starting to believe in fate. First, Aditi and her blog, now this. He smiled humourlessly. The first was certainly more pleasant than the latter.

"What are they learning now?" he asked the old man beaming by his side.

Prasad Sir took a student's Physics text book and handed it to Sanjay. "We only coach Inter first and second year students. These are the Inter second year students. It's a crucial year for them. They are trying to pass the exam privately because they work during the day."

Sanjay glanced through the text-book. "How are electro-magnetic waves propagated in the atmosphere?" he asked the student sitting on the first bench. The student looked at him blankly and then turned to Prasad Sir.

The professor looked embarrassed. "They can read and write in English but they don't understand spoken English very well," said Prasad Sir. He repeated the question slowly. The student wrote the answer down on a piece of paper and handed it over to Sanjay. It was written in perfect English.

Sanjay looked at the old man in amazement and groaned inwardly. "How am I supposed to teach them if they don't speak English very well?"

"You have to explain slowly with some Telugu words thrown in and give them notes in English. They are bright, hard-working children. They'll manage the rest. They just need a little bit of attention. It's not so difficult."

"But that's so wrong. Who's going to hire them if they don't speak English?" Sanjay stuck his hands in his pockets and thought about what lay ahead for him. A few months ago he was single and jobless. Now he had a crazy fiancée who nagged and cried and two jobs that he had to learn from the bottom-up. He needed a drink but the crazy fiancée wouldn't let him do that either.

"How can I do this, Aditi?" he was saying later that evening when they were having dinner with Mayank and Jayshree. He took a tiny sip of his whisky and let the liquid roll on his tongue for as long as possible. He was beginning to appreciate the flavour more, now that he was drinking less. "It's crazy. They don't even speak English properly. What's the point of studying science and not knowing English? Where will they get jobs? Who's going to hire them?"

"It'll be tough in the beginning but once you get used to it everything will fall into place. I can't believe you're so nervous about this. I could help them with their English. We'll all help, right?" she asked Mayank and Jayshree.

"Sure. I always wanted to teach. Do you mind if I come over?" asked Jayshree tentatively. "I'm kind of looking for a change with the baby coming."

"Hey!" protested Mayank. "You're stealing my priced employee."

"Teaching will be more flexible with the baby, Mayank," said Jayshree.

"I was just joking," said Mayank, putting his hand over Jayshree's. "I was thinking of dropping the Bay Networks project you were in charge of, anyway. The baby will give us enough sleepless nights. We don't need them from our clients. We have two new projects now. We should be fine." Sanjay and Aditi exchanged glances. Aditi couldn't believe there was a time that she actually thought that Mayank and Jayshree were boring. Now when she looked at them all she saw were two people in love.

Jayshree dug inside her purse and brought out a small black and white scrap of paper. "Look. The baby." Both parents looked at it with pride. Sanjay and Aditi looked at the piece of paper. They searched for the baby.

"Is this it?" asked Aditi pointing to a white spot.

Jayshree frowned. "I think maybe that's it," she said pointing to a slightly bigger white spot.

Sanjay stared intently at the black and white printout. There were many white spots. How many babies was Jayshree carrying anyway? Suddenly, he wanted some white spots of his own. He looked at Aditi. She had agreed to marry him but she was in no particular hurry to set a date. He always needed to steer her in the right direction. Aditi would never be in a hurry to get married. "So when do I get to meet your parents, Aditi?" he asked drily.

Aditi looked surprised. "What? Oh right. If we get married, you'll have to meet them right? How about this Sunday?"

Sanjay was pleased. "Sunday sounds great."

MEETING THE PARENTS

"**M**adam, there's a man outside who's come to see you," said the receptionist interrupting Aditi's daydreaming. She was going to introduce Sanjay to her parents today and she was feeling a little tense.

"I wonder who it is," murmured Aditi as she stepped out into the reception area carefully keeping her fingers separated so that she did not smudge her nail polish when she walked. Sanjay was standing impatiently in the reception.

Aditi gave a horrified little yelp when she saw Sanjay. Sanjay just stared at her in fascination. She was wearing a blue robe which the parlour had provided along with a yellow plastic cape and fuzzy pink slippers. A green seaweed face pack was smeared on her face, neck and arms and her hair was drenched in a foul-smelling lotion and pulled down straight all around her face. Sanjay continued looking at her for a few minutes more. Then his shoulders started shaking. He sat down on the sofa and buried his face in his hands while his shoulders continued to shake.

"Are you feeling okay? Do you want some water," she asked concerned as she sat down next to him.

"I...I'm..." he said as he shook his head and buried his face in his hands again. He looked like he was gasping for air. His shoulders shook for a few minutes more. Aditi looked at him anxiously till she realized he was laughing.

"You're laughing at me?" she asked incredulously. She was getting mad because she had thought he was having a heart attack or a fit. "I'm not so beautiful now, am I?"

"You're always beautiful," he said, eyes dancing with amusement. "It just looks like you fell into a giant bucket of green paint."

"Don't laugh. You could use a facial and hair spa. Your skin's too rough and your hair is thinning at the temples," she said crossly. "See this?" She stroked his cheek. His rough, stubbly cheeks were actually kind of nice, she thought. She had to force herself to stop stroking his cheek.

Sanjay immediately stopped laughing and touched his hair alarmed. He was losing quite a bit of hair and was shocked that Aditi had noticed.

"Why did you come here? I told you I'll meet you at *Waterfront*," she demanded, trying to stop thinking about how nice his rough cheeks felt. "Don't you know you should never visit a girl in the beauty parlour? Horrible things happen here that will keep you awake at night for a week."

"I was going to but your mom told me you were here. So I thought I would surprise you. But, boy, did you surprise me," he said beginning to laugh again. He quickly stopped when he saw her mutinous expression.

"I'll be busy here for another two hours. So there's no point waiting for me. We were supposed to meet my parents for lunch not breakfast," she said miffed.

"I know but I thought we could we talk about what we should discuss with your parents before we meet them," he said nervously.

"What's there to discuss? What did we discuss when we went to meet your aunt?" she asked confused.

"This is different," he mumbled like a sulky child. "I don't know whether they'll like me."

"Don't be ridiculous. My parent's have been trying to get me married off for years now. They don't care who I marry. They are just waiting to hand me over to some unsuspecting fool. Now go away. It's going to take me another two hours here," she said and flounced into the inner sanctum of the spa.

"Two hours," he fumed. What was he supposed to do for two hours? Was she getting a new face or what, he wondered. She didn't have time to spend with him but she had three hours to spend in the beauty palour. He opened Ms Loveleen's Blog and started a new thread in the forum. "WHY DO WOMEN SPEND SO MUCH TIME, ENERGY AND MONEY IN THE BEAUTY PARLOUR, MS LOVELEEN? SHOULDN'T THEY BE DOING SOMETHING MORE PRODUCTIVE IN THEIR LIVES?" he queried. He hoped Ms Loveleen/Aditi would respond. He was interested in what she had to say. He sat down on a sofa and pondered about how his life has changed so dramatically. He was actually going to wait for a girl in a beauty parlour for two hours.

"Do you have anything for falling hair," he finally asked the receptionist when he got tired of waiting. The receptionist smiled and handed him a thick menu of all the treatments that would stop his hair from falling.

Two hours later, Aditi was sitting with Sanjay and her mom at *Waterfront*. It was Sanjay's favourite restaurant because the high ceiling and low lighting gave it a quiet and intimate ambience. Leave him in the middle of a jungle in the dead of night and he would probably be as happy as clam. Or would that be happy as a monkey? Were monkey's happy animals, she wondered. She would have to google that.

She couldn't believe she was finally going to introduce Sanjay to her parents after much goading from both Sanjay and her parents' side. Aditi's father was yet to join them. He was still busy with an emergency surgery but he was expected to join them soon. The three of them were trying to pass the time by discussing the menu.

"What'll you have, *Aai*?" asked Aditi perusing the menu. Normally, she loved the Chinese food in this restaurant, but she wasn't feeling very hungry today. Even though this was just a casual lunch, there was no doubt that there was some serious discussion going to take place. She hoped Sanjay got along with her dad. Her father was opinionated and conservative and Sanjay, though polite, was no pushover.

Sanjay looked up and smiled at her reassuringly. In that heart-melting way that he did when he knew that she was freaking out. He was so sweet when he wasn't always trying to prove he was smarter than her. She felt a rush of love for him. This was definitely the grown up thing to do. The days of hiding under tables and lurking behind pillars were finally over.

She watched as her father made his way across the restaurant to their table. When he approached the table Sanjay stood up to shake his hand. "Well, finally you guys get to meet the great Sanjay," said Aditi nervously. What was she saying? She sounded so stupid.

"Yes. My wife has praised you so much. I was very eager to meet you after our talk that day. Of course at that time I had no idea that Aditi was interested in getting married to you. Otherwise, I would have made an effort to keep in touch. We have been trying so long to get her married off, but she never likes anybody for more than two months. There was Ayush when she returned from Dubai. Very nice boy. Don't know why she didn't like him. She even went out with Rohit Kelkar, you know, the cricketer. I thought that one would definitely last. And this boy used to keep visiting us. What was his name Umesh? Ramesh...What was his name?" He turned to his wife questioningly.

Aditi's mother was too busy trying to control her irritation to answer his question. She looked at Sanjay apologetically and fired off something in rapid Marathi that made Aditi giggle. The three of them went back and forth in Marathi. All Sanjay could fathom were random names that were thrown about. Nikhil...Amar...even a Yusuf and a John. It was nice to know that Aditi did not discriminate on the basis of religion. That was nine names and they hadn't even ordered yet. He knew that Aditi had a lot of boyfriends but hearing their names made it even more real now.

"Sorry," whispered Aditi anxiously, while her parents were busy arguing. "Are we scaring you off?"

"Not yet," he whispered back. "Is this it? Or does it get worse."

"Maybe a little worse before it gets better. Getting cold feet?" she teased. "Don't worry. You're getting the benefit of all my years of experience. I'll make it up to you later." She patted his leg.

"You better," he said grumpily, but he didn't move away.

Radhika turned back to Sanjay apologetically. "Sorry. We're so rude. But we are always so worried about Aditi. She is so stubborn and choosy and she doesn't listen to anybody. You've been with her the longest and you want to get married to her. There's no point hiding anything from you. But we're very worried about her. People talk, you know. I sometimes don't know what I've done wrong in raising her. Maybe if I'd been at home more..." she trailed off.

"Mom. You don't have to apologize for me and you don't have to feel bad about having a career," said Aditi aghast.

"It's those stupid books that she writes. It puts all kinds of useless thoughts in her head so then she behaves like her actions have no consequences. In our society how is it possible to behave like a Hollywood movie star? One day it's Tom the next day it's Harry. Have you ever read any of her books? Totally useless," Aditi's dad complained.

"We decided that we should be totally honest with you before the two of you get married. If someone says something to you later, we don't want there to be any problems," said her mother worriedly.

Sanjay felt sorry for Aditi parents. "I already know everything. Er...um...nobody cares about all those things nowadays," he said uncomfortably. He didn't know what else to say to them. He was beginning to get irritated and he didn't know why. Aditi had never hid her past from him, but the thought of Aditi with other guys never failed to make his blood boil.

"You wanted to meet my parents. Are you happy now?" said Aditi unhappily.

"Yeah. It's my fault for wanting to meet your parents," replied Sanjay stiffly without looking at her. "Can we order now?"

The rest of the lunch passed by uneventfully, Both Aditi and her father were on their best behaviour. They even managed to agree on a wedding date in four months. Plans were made to meet Sanjay's aunt and finalize the date with a priest.

After lunch, Aditi parents asked her to come home with them but she refused. She wanted to speak with Sanjay. He appeared distant and preoccupied and not at all like his usual easy-going self. It worried her.

"Why didn't you go home with your parents?" he asked curtly on the drive to his house.

"I wanted to be with you. Why? Did you want me to leave?" she said hurt.

"It's not about me. They were hurt that you didn't go home with them. How can you not see that? Would it kill you to make them happy once in a while? You're always going on and on about helping other people. Can't you see how your behaviour is affecting your parents?" he asked.

"You don't have parents who are constantly breathing down your neck so don't presume you know how to deal with them. How I act with my folks is my problem, not yours," she said rudely and instantly wished she hadn't. Sanjay didn't reply. He was looking straight ahead. His face was unreadable but he was pressing his lips tightly together. The rest of the drive was conducted in silence.

THE THREE LITTLE WORDS

When they reached home, Lakshmi was busy in the balcony. She was trimming the dead leaves from the plants. On seeing the two of them she stopped what she was doing and came up to Sanjay to ask him what to make for dinner. She looked at the two of them sprawled on the sofas at opposite ends of the living room with stormy looks on their faces and quickly backtracked to the kitchen.

"What now? You're never talking to me again? I'm sorry about what I said about your parents," she said after a while.

"Why? It's pretty much like all the other crap that you say without thinking. It's your right to say and do whatever you please, isn't it?" he said coldly.

"Why don't you tell me what's really bothering you?" she said testily.

"Nothing is bothering me. I'm just amazed at your selfishness and immaturity. How can you be so reckless with people's feelings? You go around with whoever you please without thinking of the consequences. You can be rude to your parents because they don't agree with your point of view. You can tell a whole bunch of lies because that's so much easier to do than facing the truth. None of the normal rules of behaviour apply to you, right?" he said bitterly.

"I knew it. You're just like any other guy. You're upset that I've been enjoying my life when I should have been sitting at home waiting for my prince charming to come along. You had no problem sleeping with me when you wanted to but now that we are getting married, my past is a problem for you," she said furiously.

"Is that how you think I am? You think I'm angry because of all those other guys?" he yelled even though he knew that was the case. Just thinking about what Aditi must have done with all of them was making the synapses in his brain snap with fury.

"Aren't you?" she asked.

He thought about how he was feeling and what he should say to Aditi without blowing the whole situation out of proportion. He sighed. "Okay. Your flings do bother me. I'm just trying to understand why you do what you do. Don't you care about what people think of you? At least you should care about how your parents feel? Your behaviour is making them crazy. How come you don't see that?"

"But you knew about all this before. Why is it upsetting you now? Unless you're just trying to find excuses to break up," she stated mutinously.

"If I was finding excuses to break up, why would I meet with your parents to set a wedding date?" he said quietly. "I'm just trying to understand. Do you have such low self-esteem that..."

Aditi felt the blood rushing to her head. Of all the chauvinistic things to say, she thought furiously. "I like to be around good-looking men. They keep asking me out. Why should I refuse? It's fun and flattering. What is so hard for you to understand? Don't men like to be with beautiful girls? Nobody asks them why they do what they do. You were involved with Sheetal. You even lived with her and went on holidays together. I never gave you a hard time about about it," she said tears prickling her eyes. She wiped them away with her hands.

"I'm not trying to be difficult," he said tightly. "I'm trying to understand you. Tomorrow you might get bored of me, make some excuse and dump me too."

"You know very well I won't," she defended herself.

"How am I supposed to know?" he snarled. "You keep saying you want to get married because I want to. What does that mean, Aditi? Are you doing me a favour by getting married to me? There's no need. There are plenty of women who'll gladly marry me."

"Then do that. Everybody in this world is free to do whatever they like. Go marry some virgin. That way you won't have to wonder all the time if some other guy was better than you," she screamed, waving her hands around. "I think marriage is just a piece of paper, but it's important to you so it's fine with me. I don't know what is so difficult to understand about that? Have you ever thought that maybe I hadn't met anyone special enough to try to make it work before? I'm trying so hard to make it work with you but you haven't noticed that, have you?" She could feel tears flowing down her cheeks and didn't want to cry in front of Sanjay. She stomped upstairs towards the bedroom and locked it behind her.

He could hear her sobbing inside the bedroom but he was too angry and exhausted to speak to Aditi. A subdued Lakshmi came up to him and asked him what he wanted to have for dinner. He waved her off and asked her to go home. When she was leaving she sniffed superciliously and gave him a five-minute lecture about how he was treating Aditi. Stupid woman. Who told her she could give him advice about his love life? He stretched out on the sofa and thought about what Aditi said. How did it matter what her reasons were to get married. They were getting married and she said that she loved him. What more did he want, he asked himself. He couldn't believe Sheetal's infidelity had made him so insecure.

It was dark when he was woken up by an anxious Aditi crouching next to him. He had fallen asleep on the couch. They hadn't even had dinner. He sat up and yawned.

"I fell asleep. You have to drop me home," she said in a soft voice. Her face looked swollen and her eyes were red and puffy.

"Adi, I'm sorry," he said gruffly. He cupped her face with his hand and touched the corner of her eye gently with his thumb. She closed her eyes. He tried to pull her into his arms but she resisted.

"I really want to go," she said stiffly.

"You cry so much. How come you don't get dehydrated?" he asked softly. He sat down on the floor and pulled her to him again. This time she went into his arms willingly. He hugged her tight. Her ribs felt like they might crack but she didn't protest. "Are you going to cry all the time after we're married?"

"You still want to get married," she asked shocked. She didn't think two people could stay together after having such an ugly fight. But apparently Sanjay did.

"Yeah. Why? Don't you?" he asked surprised.

"After everything that happened? I thought you don't want to see me anymore. You were so angry," she said confused.

"I don't think it's going to be the last time that we fight. But I still love you," he said amused.

Aditi froze. "What did you just say?" she asked, a smile spreading slowly across her face.

"I said it won't be the last time we fight," he said, recognizing his slip.

"And after that? I want you to say it, Sanjay," Aditi said mulishly. "I need to hear it."

"Okay fine. I love you," said Sanjay getting up and walking towards the kitchen. He checked the fridge for something to eat. There was nothing. He sighed and opened a packet of dried pasta.

"Could you say it like you mean it? Atleast once in your whole life?" she whined.

"Why?" asked Sanjay exasperated. "It's not me. I don't buy flowers and mushy cards. I don't say 'I love you' all the time. I don't care about Valentine's Day. It's just not my thing."

Aditi gave up. There was no point pushing him. Anyway, romance wasn't in those three little words. It was in all the things somebody did to make you feel special and Sanjay did plenty of that. "Okay. I get it. Just like getting a marriage certificate doesn't mean anything to me. I'm still getting married because you want to, but if you expect me to be the typical, traditional wife, I won't do it. I can't change who I am when I'm with you. I have to be me or it won't work. Do you get it?" She walked up to him and looked up at him earnestly.

Sanjay stared back at her. "So basically you just want all the fun of being married without the responsibilities. Fine," he said slowly. "I never asked you to change for me, Adi. We both want to be together. We just have different ways of expressing it." He added the pasta to the water. "And since we're clearing the air today, I think I should tell you, that I'm very possessive about what's mine. I won't take it if guys like Sharad are hanging around you all the time after we're married."

"That's crazy," said Aditi astounded. "You can't tell me who I can or cannot be friends with."

"I'm not telling you who to make friends with. I just don't want you hanging around any guys when I'm not around. And I want to know who you're with all the time." He looked at Aditi glaring at him and tried pleading. "You have to give me this one thing Adi. Why can't you ever listen to anything I say? Can't you at least pretend to be submissive once in a while?" he said sulkily.

"If I pretend to be submissive, you'll have to pretend to be manly. You think you can manage that?" she said teasingly.

Sanjay face turned to stone. He turned off the gas and came striding towards her. Aditi didn't like the look in his eyes. She knew she had pushed him too far. "What did you say?" he asked. She backed up against the wall as Sanjay came and stood in front of her. "Just because I let you have your own way all the time, don't think I'm a fool, Adi."

"Okay. Okay. I just said I better not catch you even smiling at another girl," she amended quickly, her heart pounding loudly.

He looked amused. "You know that would never happen. You're the one with admirers hanging around all the time. You walk into a room and all the guys start staring. Why didn't you try to be a movie star?"

"It's just the outside package. It doesn't mean anything. Nobody makes me feel like you do," said Aditi.

"How do I make you feel?" he asked confused. "I don't really know. You don't want the security of being married. What are you getting out of this? I used to worry that somebody might marry me only for the money, but you want nothing and somehow that irritates me now. I want to give you everything, but you don't want it."

"I want you. That's all." She turned to the pasta he had made. "And you're a good cook. I always wanted a guy who could cook. Let's eat." She didn't want to fight anymore. It was exhausting and a waste of time.

They walked to the kitchen. Aditi took out plates and set the table. Sanjay smiled but he was still subdued. "Stay the night, Adi. You haven't stayed with me since Phuket. It gets really lonely sometimes."

"Didn't you just lecture me about not worrying my parents?" complained Aditi.

"Call them. You've worried them so much already. A little more won't hurt," he said softly, taking her in his arms.

Aditi melted. "It must get boring for you after a while staring at the walls all by yourself. Why don't you ever get in touch with any of your relatives or make some new friends? You're so anti-social."

"I thought we have already been through this. I don't connect with them anymore. I know who all really care for me and that's enough." He went upto the stove and took a spoon to taste the sauce. He added some oregano. He took another spoonful of the sauce and blew on it to cool it down before feeding it to Aditi who came and stood next to him.

"Um. Good. I've got an idea. Since you're dying to do something for me, I have a small favour to ask you. Can we cancel that huge wedding that my parents are planning?" she said seriously and watched the smile vanish from his face.

"Why?" he asked stunned.

"I just want to have a small wedding with close friends and family. I can't go through that nonsense again. I promised myself I would never plan that kind of wasteful wedding again. Do you mind?" she asked.

"Okay. That's fine," he said smiling with relief. "I thought you didn't want to have a wedding at all. Won't your parents mind?"

"You don't worry about my parents," she said confidently.

"I don't care about the wedding as long as we're getting married," he replied, serving them both the pasta.

They were the sweetest words Aditi had ever heard. She did a little dance all around the kitchen. She stopped when she found Sanjay staring at her. She went and sat at the dining table, trying to look dignified.

WEDDING WOES

Sanjay woke up the next day to Aditi's cheerful voice. He tried to put an arm around her only to encounter something plastic, cool and heavy lying on top of her. He opened one eye. Aditi was sitting up with her laptop and a cup of black tea.

"Sleepyhead just woke up," he heard her saying. He opened the other eye to see Sheetal on the screen.

"Hi Sanjay. You look like you've been well fucked," Sheetal's image told him cheerfully.

"Shit. Are you on Skype with Sheetal?" he sat up and hurriedly covered himself. What was the matter with Aditi? She had no concept of privacy. She was sitting in front of his ex-girlfriend wearing nothing but his old T-shirt and discussing him as if he wasn't there. He surreptitiously covered her bare legs with the comforter.

"No need to be embarrassed Sanjay. There's nothing I haven't seen before, right?" asked Sheetal. She seemed in an irritatingly good mood, thought Sanjay unhappily. "Anyway, Sharad is atleast ten times more ripped than you. He has a six-pack, did you know? I never thought I'll ever be able to see one of those."

"Well, lucky you, Sheetal. I'm glad you found what you're looking for. Especially after that big lecture you gave me about airheads," replied Sanjay sarcastically. He could get a six-pack too, he thought self-consciously. If he sucked in his stomach tight there was a discernable six-pack buried somewhere in his abdomen. He just wasn't one of those brawny types like Sharad who were obsessed with finding it.

"Don't mind him. He's a little grumpy this morning. We were up till late last night," said Aditi. "What was that about airheads?"

"Nothing," said both Sanjay and Sheetal guiltily. Sheetal glared at Sanjay through the screen.

"It's better to get him to bed early, Aditi. If it were up to him, he'll sleep at three in the morning everyday. It's not good for his health but he won't listen," advised Sheetal sympathetically. "If he's up till midnight, give him a little snack. That sometimes makes him drowsy."

"I'll try. It's still all new to me," said Aditi apologetically.

Sanjay looked at the two of them like they had gone crazy. "As much as I'm enjoying this discussion, I think it time for you to go, Sheetal," he said closing the laptop. "Are you insane? Do you miss having a mother-in-law? Talk to Attamma. Why have you adopted Sheetal?"

"She's nice. Attamma only knows the kiddy you. She doesn't really know the grown up you," said Aditi. "Sheetal really cares about you. Why didn't you two get married? You two are so perfect for each other. Was the sex bad?" Sanjay shot her a don't-go-there look so she changed tack. "Yesterday, you said you want to understand me. Today, I want to understand you. Why live together? Why not just get married?"

"I told you. We would have married if she hadn't cheated on me,"said Sanjay. "And I used to be really busy. What part don't you understand?"

"You didn't find time in five years?" she said disbelievingly. "You know, we're not that different. You didn't want to be tied down either."

"There's a big difference between the twenties and thirties. My priorities have changed," he said heading to the bathroom. Aditi leaned back and enjoyed the view. He was just wearing shorts that were hanging really low on his hips. She could enjoy this view every morning, she realized happily. Sanjay was right. It would be nicer when they got married.

"We were just discussing the wedding. Sheetal is so excited. She's planning on coming down to Hyderabad in two weeks to meet Sharad, so she might be able to attend the wedding if we have it then. Won't that be great?" Aditi announced excitedly.

Sanjay turned. "No, that would not be great, Adi. I do not want Sheetal at our wedding," Sanjay growled. "Are you planning on inviting all your exes to the wedding?"

"No. Of course not. I don't even know where half of them are. But Sheetal is like part of your family. Besides, she'll be with Sharad. We have to invite her." Sanjay just shook his head and muttered under his breath in Telugu banging the bathroom door loudly.

"You know that's not very polite. If you're going to curse me you should atleast do it in a language I understand," she yelled but she was smiling.

When Sanjay emerged from the bathroom freshly showered and shaved, Aditi was still lying in bed. "Aren't you getting dressed? I have to drop you at your parent's place before I go to work," he said worriedly, already preoccupied. He went to his cupboard and took out a white shirt and grey trousers.

Aditi liked the way he said 'parent's place' like this was already her house. "If that's my parent's place where's my place?" she asked naughtily.

Sanjay put on his trousers and grinned at her. He opened the two cupboards next to his own and opened it. They were empty. "That's your place. Now get up. I'm getting late." He threw his towel at her. Aditi hugged it even though it was damp. It smelt of him.

"Why don't you take the day off? We can plan the wedding," she suggested. Before he could answer, his Blackberry buzzed and he rushed to the bedside to answer it. He tucked his shirt into his pants with his phone tucked in awkwardly between his shoulder and ear. "Has Mohan come? Is it working now?" he asked whoever was on the other side of the call.

Aditi sighed and searched for his headset. She went up to him and gave it to him. He shot her a grateful smile and walked out of the room. This was the flipside of what she had to look forward too, she realized. She turned around and went to shower.

When Aditi emerged from the bedroom and came downstairs, Sanjay had already brewed some coffee and was making dosas from the batter that Lakshmi had stored in the fridge. "Do you want some?" he asked turning around.

Aditi's stomach rumbled. The fragrance of the brewed coffee intermingling with that of the crisping dosa smelt delicious. "Thanks. I'll have one," she said guiltily. Sanjay waited on her hand and foot whenever she was here. She had to start doing some work around here. She didn't want him to treat her like a guest. If she wasn't going to behave like his personal maid, she had no right to expect him to be hers. She hugged him from behind and rested her head on his shoulder. "What time does Lakshmi come in? You make your own breakfast every morning?" He did this alone everyday? No wonder he wanted to get married.

"Yes. She'll be here by ten. She stays till seven. She has her own key. Lata comes at eleven. She does the cleaning and stuff. She leaves at three," he said as Aditi continued to hold on to him like she was drowning. She was very affectionate in the mornings. It took some getting used to...especially when he was getting late for work. He usually started checking his emails while having breakfast but he didn't think Aditi would appreciate it very much. "What?" he asked indulgently as Aditi began to kiss him. "Adi," he protested turning off the gas. His arms went around her. He didn't think there was going to be time for breakfast.

"So you'll come sari-shopping with me in the afternoon? We can have lunch together," said Aditi when they were finally in the car.

"I have a business lunch this afternoon," he said cautiously. He didn't think he wanted to go sari-shopping even he was free but he didn't think it was wise to tell Aditi that. "Why don't I get you an add-on credit card? Then you can do whatever shopping you like."

"How about this evening? Will you be free then?" she asked hopefully.

"Er...I'm going to the gym and then I have class in the evenings, remember?" he replied.

Sanjay knew Aditi was annoyed. He had developed a radar that instantly detected the exact moment that Aditi was upset with him. The only problem was that he couldn't always tell what it was that she was annoyed about. Anything could set her off. He didn't want to upset her right now. Nobody argues with a woman who had just given a mind-numbing blow job. He would skip breakfast for it any day.

"And what about our wedding?" she said shortly. "Don't you want to be involved in anything?" She felt herself getting depressed. She couldn't understand how Sanjay just switched off after they had been so intimate. Sanjay was turning out to be exactly like all the other guys she had met before. Now that he knew that she loved him and was totally committed to him, he had better things to do.

"I thought we agreed we would have a simple wedding with only our close friends and family present. Isn't that what you wanted?" he reminded her gently. "How much preparation does that need? We'll have it in a hotel. They have event managers who arrange everything. All we have to do is decide the menu and decorations. There's plenty of time for that." He patted her arm like she was a little child and she felt herself melting a bit. This sleeping-over stuff was dangerous. She felt too content to argue with him strenuously. Is this how she was going to feel all the time after they were married, she wondered anxiously.

"Why don't we have it at *Hyatt*? We can go there tomorrow and fix the menu? We can have dinner there," he said trying to make peace. He didn't mind menu planning. That was one area he was comfortable with.

"Just because a hotel can arrange everything, that doesn't mean that we shouldn't discuss anything," she argued. "Is this how you want it? You're just going to meet me at the wedding venue in your suit. Not a suit. You can't wear a suit for the ceremony. We don't even know what you're wearing for the wedding. How can we have a wedding in two weeks?" she said in a panic.

"Calm down. It takes two hours to buy an outfit. Why don't you go buy me one when you're done with the sari-shopping?" he said brightly.

Because I want you to come with me, she wanted to scream at him. Obviously his idea of arranging a wedding was to hand out the cash while she did the running around. He probably learnt that management technique while he was doing his Ph.D., she thought sarcastically. "So you'll wear whatever I get you?" she asked, her voice dangerously soft. "And I can have any type of ceremony I want?"

"Sure," he said confidently but alarm bells were ringing in his head. He pictured himself in a green sherwani with belly dancers shaking their hips around the mantap. She wouldn't do that to him, would she? Aditi's tastes ranged from haute couture to downright risqué depending on her mood. He never knew what to expect from her. It was exciting…some of the time. "So long as it's on the sober side," he added hastily.

"Fine," she said with false enthusiasm. "I'll go everywhere by myself and you can do whatever you want." She looked at him. He looked smug. Like he had solved a big world crisis.

She wanted to make him squirm a bit. "You know Jamaal wouldn't do something like this," she said seriously.

"Who the hell is Jamaal?" he asked wearily, rubbing the back of his neck.

"He's the Arab sheikh in this short story I'm writing," she informed him.

Sanjay laughed. That was one less ex-boyfriend to deal with. "Of course he wouldn't do anything that you didn't like. You created him. He's a slave of your imagination. I'm not." He stopped outside her house and tapped his fingers impatiently on the steering wheel. He still looked annoyingly smug.

"Fine. But if you're good, I'll let you do me on your desk in your office," she whispered naughtily in his ear.

Sanjay's eyes widened. The smug look was gone. "That sounds so freaking hot. How do you do that?" he groaned. He didn't think he could stop thinking about it now…especially when he was at work.

"Go to work," she said kissing him gently. She got out of the car. Who was a slave of her imagination now, she thought amused. She looked at her house guiltily. She needed to think of something imaginative to tell her parents or she would be in a lot of trouble.

WHEN CULTURES COLLIDE

Aditi walked into Sanjay's office three days later to find him leaning back in his chair, talking on the phone. Mohit, Shruti and Rohan were sitting on a couch nearby working out Maths exercises. "Good afternoon, Madam," they wished her together.

"Good afternoon," she wished them back and looked at Sanjay questioningly. He smiled at her and continued to speak on the phone. She went up to him and kissed him on the forehead. He straightened abruptly and reddened. She heard a few giggles from the couch. She settled herself on a chair opposite Sanjay. He hung up. "I gave them jobs here. They weren't able to study when they were working all day," he said sheepishly.

"And what work do they do here all day?" she teased.

"Study and fetch me tea and coffee," he replied.

"That's so sweet, Sanjay." She rose to give him a hug but sat down again when Sanjay eyed her apprehensively.

"Ready to leave?" asked Sanjay. They had been invited to

Mayank's house for lunch because Jayshree's parents had come for a visit.

"Do you want to take my car?" asked Aditi. Sanjay imagined sitting in her tiny car and shuddered. He needed to buy Aditi a proper car. The stronger the better. Maybe a Unimog or a Hummer, he thought grinning.

"Why are you smiling?" asked Aditi.

"I was imagining you in a monster truck," he replied.

Aditi looked at him sadly. "Most men imagine women in lingerie," she muttered.

"We'll take my car," he said quickly. He turned to the children. "Do you need me to drop you back home?"

"No. We'll go back by bus, Sir. No problem," said Mohan. They gathered up their books. They were passing through the office when Mohan waved excitedly at Sanjay from behind a glass window. Sanjay stepped into the room to see what had got his CTO so excited. Aditi and the children exchanged puzzled glances.

"We'll leave Madam," they said and went off leaving Aditi alone. Aditi sighed and trudged back to Sanjay's office.

Inside the room, Mohan demonstrated their latest trend-analysis software. "We managed to increase the accuracy of the algorithm by 5 percent," beamed Mohan. Mohan demonstrated the software and both Sanjay and Mohan gazed at the screen like proud parents who suddenly realized that they had produced a child prodigy.

Sanjay played with the software for a while. He punched in different numbers and checked the charts that the system created. He noted some other problems and got into a lengthy discussion with Mohan. "We need to set up a meeting with John this evening to keep him updated about the progress."

"I'll set it up for seven. Is that okay with you?" asked Mohan.

"Sounds good. Aren't you leaving for lunch?" asked Sanjay when his own rumbled in protest. Lunch. Aditi. Damn, he thought. "I need to go. I'll see you later."

He rushed out of the room. He peeked into his office. Aditi was sitting on the couch listening to her iPod. "Sorry," he said contritely. "I lost track of time."

"So what's new?" replied Aditi resigned.

When they walked into Mayank and Jayshree's house some time later, they were in for a shock. The entire ambience of the house had changed. It now resembled a mini Madurai. All Mayank's whiskies, rums and vodkas were cleared from the bar and photos of Venkateshwara, Lakshmi and Saraswati were placed in its place. The bar had doubled up as a pooja room. M. L. Vasanthakumari crooned softly in the background and the fragrant aroma of *sambar* mixed with incense from the morning pooja wafted around the room. A pure vegetarian, South Indian meal had been served.

"Very good *koottu*, Jayshree," said Jayshree's father, beaming at Jayshree. Gopal Sastri was always beaming at his daughter. As far as he was concerned the sun rose and set with Jayshree. They normally visited only for a couple of weeks every year, but it usually felt like a lifetime to Mayank.

Koottu. So that's what this weird combination of dal and vegetables is called, thought Mayank fascinated. He pushed aside the vegetables that Jayshree had served him and reluctantly ate the *sambar* and rice. He was not a big fan of South Indian food. Especially vegetarian South Indian food. He wondered when Jayshree was going to stand up to her parents and admit that she had been eating non-vegetarian food for almost six years now and drank like a fish. The only time she bothered to perform pooja in the morning was when her parents were around. He felt despondent. It was going to be a long couple of weeks.

"Uncle, you must be so excited about the baby," said Aditi.

"Yes. Yes. It's all by God's grace. We were all wondering why there was no good news from Jayshree's side. Nowadays, with all this fast-paced, high-society life, people don't want a baby to ruin their lifestyle," replied Jayshree's dad giving Mayank a quick glance.

"Well, Jayshree was not ready to have a baby till recently," said Mayank defensively. His father-in-law had made it sound like Jayshree had begged him to make her pregnant but he had somehow refused to part with his sperm. The image made him smile. He looked at Jayshree to see if she had anything to add. She was looking down like a pious, dutiful daughter. She was such a good actress sometimes.

"But now we are all very happy," added Jayshree's mother quickly. "Vidya has even looked for a good doctor for the delivery." Vidya was Jayshree's brother's wife. She was an ophthalmologist in Chennai.

"Why has Vidya looked for a doctor in Chennai?" asked Mayank confused.

"The first delivery is always in the parent's house, no? We have to take Jayshree home," Jayshree's father informed Mayank like he was a bit slow.

"You're not having the baby here?" Mayank asked Jayshree.

"I thought you understood. All women have their first child in their parent's place. Don't you remember Anju went off to Meerut for four months during her delivery?" said Jayshree.

"But if you go to Chennai for the delivery then I can't be there for you during the labour," said Mayank testily. Sanjay and Aditi looked at Jayshree and then concentrated on their food.

"Why do you want to be with Jayshree during the labour?" asked Jayshree mother horrified. "A pregnant woman needs her mother not her husband. Husbands can't give the same care and support like a mother."

"It's no big deal, Mayank. The moment Shree goes into labour, she'll give you a call. You can take the next flight to Madras and go straight to the hospital and be with her," said Aditi trying to pacify him.

"Isn't it a good thing? You get a nice, beautiful baby without going through the gruesome part," said Sanjay consolingly.

"I guess," said Mayank looking at Jayshree who was avoiding his gaze. He was a bit hurt that Jayshree had not defended him after her mother claimed that husbands didn't support and care for their wives like their mother's did. They had been through so much together. He didn't recall her mother rushing to support them every time they had a crisis.

Jayshree got up to serve the *payasam* that she had made. "No. No. You sit. You've done enough work already. Now you relax," her mother admonished. She left to serve the sweet dish. Jayshree's father got up to watch the television, leaving the four of them alone on the dining table.

Jayshree sat down and glanced at Mayank. "This is how it is in India, Mayank. We have to follow the customs, right?" said Jayshree pleadingly.

Sanjay tasted a spoonful of Jayshree's *payasam*. It tasted fabulous. "Aren't you going to have some *payasam*?" he asked Mayank.

"I don't like it," muttered Mayank. He smiled at Jayshree. "I think you need to tell your parents about how you really want to live your life, Shree. You're going to be a mother too. Do you want our kid to tell us the truth or tell us what we want to hear?"

Jayshree felt silent. What Mayank was saying was absolutely right. What kind of mother would she be if she was still lying to her own parents? She looked up to see Aditi and Sanjay looking at her sympathetically. They probably thought she was a wimp and they would be right. She took a deep breath. "Usha, Mayank doesn't like the *koottu*, why don't you heat up some of the leftover chicken curry," said Jayshree to her maid in a scared voice.

There was pin-drop silence in the house.

"Chee! You have non-veg food in the house, Jayshree. You're a not a Brahmin anymore. How could you? You've spoilt everything," moaned her mother as Usha brought the chicken curry and served Mayank.

"You thought I had spoilt everything the day I married Mayank, so how does it matter what we eat now?" said Jayshree. "Why shouldn't Mayank have non-veg food in the house? It's his house. He's worked hard to pay for it. Why shouldn't he eat what he wants?"

Mayank looked at the chicken curry with distaste. He had lost his appetite. "I said be yourself, not give them a heart attack," he whispered.

"And I'm having the baby in Hyderabad, not in Chennai,"

she added while she was still feeling brave. "I know Aditi's mom. She's the best gynaecologist in Hyderabad. I feel comfortable with her. I don't understand why I have to go to a strange doctor picked by Vidya."

"Deal with one issue at a time, Shree. There's no need to do everything today," said Aditi soothingly.

But Jayshree was past caring now. "I don't understand why you make such a big deal about Vidya. Whenever I come there, Arvind and Vidya are so busy with their work and their friends. It's pretty obvious I'm just a guest there. Why should I have the baby there, when nobody has the time? I want to have the baby in my house. This is my house," said Jayshree stubbornly.

Mayank groaned. "I can't watch this. Aditi stop her."

"If you felt this way, you should have informed us sooner, Jayshree. I wouldn't have troubled poor Vidya to find a doctor. Poor thing works so hard. Of course, if you want to have the baby here, it's your choice. You are a grown-up now. You can make your own decisions," said Jayshree's mother curtly.

"You could come here and help me with the baby here," said Jayshree with a soft voice.

Her mother turned and looked at her. "We'll see," she said quietly and went into her room.

Mayank, Aditi and Jayshree's father looked at each other with a dazed expression. Sanjay was the only one smiling. Aditi kicked him under the table.

BACK TO THE BEGINNING

Sanjay was explaining the Doppler Effect to his class of Inter second year students when he noticed Mohan staring dreamily at a serious Shruti. He stopped mid-lecture and broke off a tiny piece of chalk and aimed it at Mohan. The chalk hit a startled Mohan on the forehead. Mohan blushed furiously when Sanjay raised his eyebrows questioningly.

"Am I boring you?" asked Sanjay annoyed.

"No Sir. Sorry Sir," muttered a flustered Mohan looking back into his notebook.

Sanjay went back to his lecture. Teenagers, he thought exasperated. He could probably get paid lots of money to teach graduate level students in some prestigious college anywhere around the world and when he was doing it for free, nobody wanted to listen. On the other hand, he couldn't really blame Mohan. If he had to choose between Aditi and the Doppler Effect, he knew what he would choose.

He finished his lecture and went into the administrative office just as Jayshree walked out of the classroom next door. They both made their way to the office.

"So are you enjoying teaching?" Sanjay asked smiling.

"Fabulous. I've never felt so great before. I don't know why I never thought of teaching before. You're a much better boss than Mayank." Sanjay laughed and leaned back in the plush, black leather chair that had been specially delivered for him yesterday. It looked completely incongruous in the old office. "And nice chair by the way. Do I get one too?"

"Sure. Take this," he said getting up. "I couldn't bear those crappy, plastic ones so Aditi bought me this. He settled himself on a plastic chair while Jayshree sank into the leather chair and put her feet up on the desk. Sanjay looked up from the schedule he was looking at and raised his eyebrows. "You're only getting away with this because you're pregnant and my most valuable employee."

Jayshree looked at him calmly. "I don't care. You don't intimidate me anymore.

"I used to intimidate you?" He looked at her with surprise.

"You used to be so driven Sanjay. Don't you remember?" asked Jayshree. "There were rumours circulating that you didn't let a team of thirty go home for a whole week when they screwed up a deadline in Paradigm and after that you sent them on an all-expense-paid trip to Hawaii for a week with their families."

"Okay. That really happened," he confessed. "And I'll do it again too. Don't worry I won't do it to you. I really appreciate what you're doing here, Jayshree. Just let me know if it's getting too much for you." Even though Aditi was good with the English course, she was terrible with the administrative work. She was also very busy with her book and other activities. Jayshree had been a big help in organizing the course work and the general functioning and repairs of the coaching centre. It was obvious to Sanjay that although Prasad Sir was a good teacher he was a horrible administrator.

"I loved how my father talked about Science and Maths in school. He is a scientist, you know. It would be nice if I could pass it on to others," she said.

It's not just about the subject matter. You are very patient with people. Mayank is lucky to have you." said Sanjay sincerely. He paused awkwardly before proceeding. "I know you didn't really want to come to India, but you did because Mayank wanted you to. You've done a really good job of adjusting here. I don't think Aditi would ever do something like that for me."

"You don't know that," said Jayshree surprised at his sudden change of topic. "You're not even married to her yet. You don't know what she'll do or not do for you. Aditi swore she would never get married but you wanted to, so she agreed. Isn't that something?"

"I guess so," he agreed reluctantly but he was not convinced. "Sometimes I feel like I've forced Aditi to get engaged and that's probably not very wise. What if she's not happy after we get married and then she leaves me?"

Jayshree frowned. She didn't know what to say about that. "I might leave Mayank tomorrow. There are no guarantees in life, Sanjay."

"There's no way you will leave Mayank nor will he ever leave you. You are the most perfectly-matched couple I have ever seen," scoffed Sanjay.

Jayshree stared at him in disbelief. "Mayank and I fight all the time. What makes you say we're the perfect couple? We come from two totally different backgrounds. Haven't you noticed?"

"But you two always manage to work it out," said Sanjay. "I hope everything turned out okay with your mom."

Jayshree blushed. "I'm sorry I made such a scene. She was horrified but she's getting used to it. Mayank and I talked a lot. We decided that we're not going to put other people's expectations before our own family anymore," said Jayshree firmly. She put her feet down and leaned forward. "You and Aditi will work things out just like we do. Aditi wants to be with you. It's the actual wedding and all the expectations related to getting married that scare her. I know you feel insecure about Aditi right now but things will change. Relationships keep changing. One day you'll be leading her. Another day Aditi will be leading you. It'll all balance out. Nobody in a real marriage feels secure all the time. Infact, I think you and Aditi are the most romantic couple I have ever seen."

"Aditi is the romantic one, not me," he mumbled embarrassed. "Okay. We should get back to work. I've prepared these notes and diagrams for all the chapters in Maths and Physics that make it easy to understand. This is how I used to study when I was in school and college. I'm not good with this Chem and Bio stuff. I need more teachers."

"A lot of my friends have stopped working after having kids. Maybe I can ask some of them if they would want to work part-time," said Jayshree brightening.

"Great. Have you seen these texts? They're terrible. You know what we should do? We should print our own material," said Sanjay enthusiastically.

Jayshree laughed. "Slow down, Hotshot. You've become used to thinking big. Think small. You don't want to confuse these kids by changing too much too soon." She became thoughtful. "You know, if you're really thinking big, we can ask around other corporates. Maybe there are other people who would want to help out. We could start a mentoring program or something."

Sanjay was thoughtful. Jayshree watched him fascinated. Aditi had informed her this morning that Sanjay had worked all night at Tangential and yet here he was bright-eyed and full of energy like it was nothing. Only somebody like Aditi could keep up with him. They were both a couple of high-energy, self-involved maniacs in their own way.

"I can't think small. That's always been my problem. It's all or nothing for me," he said grinning. "I like your idea, Jayshree. I'm thinking of moving this place into my old house. I want to have labs and stuff. These kids need to learn the concepts by doing practical stuff not just learn a bunch of prepared answers. It's no wonder they don't go far in life. They don't know why they are doing what they are doing. What do you think about working here full-time? I need somebody to head this place. You're perfect for this job."

Jayshree felt relieved to hear his offer. She was tired of software development and was looking for a change. She had been searching for something meaningful to do with her life and this sounded great. It would be easier when the baby came too. "I was wondering when you were going to offer me a job. Just let me confirm with Mayank but mostly, it's a yes." She looked over the notes and diagrams that Sanjay had prepared. "Hey! Not bad, Sanjay."

"Thanks. I know. I spent my whole childhood just studying. They better be good," he said immodestly. "I used to think if I did well, my dad would stop being sad and pay attention to me for a change." He waited for the familiar bitterness to take over whenever he thought of his father but it didn't come.

Suddenly, he understood why his father had spent so much time coaching these kids. There was a satisfaction that helping other people gave you that distracted you from your own problems. The realization stunned Sanjay. Of course his father had been lonely. A child, no matter how well-loved, was not a substitute for a spouse. How could he have been so stupid? His father had been thirty-seven when his mother had died. His father could have remarried but all he had done was coach a few kids. Why had he grudged him that?

"The only reason I studied so hard was to prove to my parents that I was career-oriented so that they wouldn't get me married off at seventeen," said Jayshree.

"Do you think that there are people who actually study for the right reasons?" Sanjay asked with a twinkle in his eye.

"I don't know. Mayank studied hard to get away from his mom." They both laughed.

"I can see that happening," said Sanjay, remembering Mayank's mom. "Maybe Aditi had the right idea. She dropped out of college and she's still doing well. She got paid fifty thousand yesterday just to dress up and go to some shop opening and cut a ribbon. Imagine somebody getting paid to attend parties." He had seen a picture of her in the society pages this morning. She was smiling into the camera with the shop owner beaming at her idiotically with his arm around her shoulders. It had taken all his self-control not to question her about it. Finally, he had dashed off a message to Ms Loveleen and Aditi had forbidden him to ever post on her website again.

"Aditi's special," said Jayshree fondly. "Not everybody can carry off everything she does."

"That's true," said Sanjay. "She is special."

CRUEL KARMA

Aditi exited from the shop and realized that it had become very late. Most of the other shops had already downed their shutters and the street wore a deserted look. She was glad she had brought a shawl with her. She wrapped it around her head and shoulders and hurried towards the well-lit main road where her car was parked.

She didn't know why but she was getting the strange feeling that she was being followed. Sometimes it was a curse to have such an active imagination. She clutched her purse closer to her body.

She had almost reached her car, when a muscular arm wrapped around her waist and lifted her off the ground. Another hand clamped around her mouth and she was unceremoniously dumped into a Ford Fortuner with darkened windows. The hoodlum had a monkey cap pulled over his face so she couldn't identify him. He tied up her hands and legs and blindfolded her. "Ouch! That hurts," she yelled. "Is this some kind of joke? Did one of my friends ask you to do this?" Her questions remained unanswered as a piece of tape was placed over her mouth and the door slammed shut.

She didn't know how long she lay sprawled on the backseat of the SUV, but her arms were beginning to ache and the skin beneath the tape was itching. She felt momentarily relieved when the SUV came to a stop and dread soon followed. What the hell was happening? Her life had slowly fallen into place. She was finally writing something meaningful. She was excited about getting married and now this had to happen.

She hoped she wasn't going to be raped and tortured. She couldn't handle pain. She looked at her plain T-shirt and jeans. She wasn't even dressed provocatively. Maybe God was punishing her for fantasising about Arab sheikhs when He had given her a perfectly good guy. She said a quick prayer telling God she was joking and she was very happy with Sanjay. She felt cold and numb.

The hoodlum opened the door and dragged her into sitting position. He untied her feet and forced her to stand and walk. They walked for a few minutes and entered an elevator. She couldn't make out which floor they got off at but it was the penthouse. After a short walk, he pushed her onto a bed. Aditi's heart sank. He's going to rape me, she thought in panic. She tried to kick and hit him, but he was too strong for her. He removed her blindfold and the tape over her mouth and untied her hands. The man left, locking the door behind him.

She was momentarily relieved but the fear came crashing back again. She wouldn't be in some strange bed if something horrible wasn't in store for her in the near future. She sank onto the bed despondently. She looked around the room. There were no windows in the small room...just some cupboards and a single bed. Why hadn't she kept her cellphone in her pocket instead of keeping it in her purse? Why hadn't she ever taken any self-defence classes?

She thought of Sanjay and tears pricked her eyes. She thought about her parents and their constant worry and nagging, their insistence to be home on time, to dress conservatively and to stay away from useless men. It all made sense now. Fresh tears poured down from her cheeks. She cried for five minutes and then checked herself. Even docile village girls got abducted sometimes. She was not going to feel sorry for how she had led her life. She had lived a full life and she was happy about it. She got up and searched the room for a means to escape.

The door opened and Aditi cringed again. She looked towards the door frightened. Ayush, her ex-boyfriend stood before her uncertainly.

All her fear vanished. "Ayush, you stupid idiot. Have you bloody lost your mind? What's the meaning of this? Let me go right now. Is this some kind of joke?" she hissed.

"I really miss you, Aditi. I really love you. More than that prissy bastard you're going out with right now," he pleaded. "What does he have that I don't? Money? I'm doing well now and my dad's rich too. I didn't tell you before but my dad's an MLA. I can do anything for you. I can give you anything you want." He ran out of steam after his impassioned speech and sat down heavily on the bed beside her.

Prissy bastard? Was he talking about Sanjay? She was terribly offended. Sanjay wasn't prissy. It was those awful Ralph Lauren polo T-shirts that he wore all the time that made him look prissy. Ayush had never seen Sanjay with his shirt off, she thought smugly. But now was not the time to think about that. "Sanjay's not prissy," she said defensively. Hope began to trickle into her heart. She watched his dejected face carefully. "So you don't want to rape me?"

He looked horrified. "Of course not. I love you, Aditi. I

want to marry you," he said mournfully. "I can make you very happy, if you'll let me. More than that stupid US-returned that you're seeing. How come you went to Phuket with him? I would have taken you to Paris if you had let me and I wouldn't have left you alone for a minute. I used to make you happy, remember? When are you planning on dumping him?"

Aditi felt ashamed. She didn't even remember what excuse she had given Ayush for breaking up with him. She was no better than all those guys she kept critizing. She had become the female version of all the guys she hated. She felt a little disgusted. "I'm not planning to dump him. I'm getting married to him. I love him."

Ayush looked at her disbelievingly. "You love him and are going to marry him? Bullshit!"

"How do you know so much about me?" she demanded.

"It's easy to keep track of people nowadays. That guy outside has been following you for months," Ayush said grinning. "How come you love him? You always liked guys who are a little crazy and twisted," he said softly.

She pushed him. "No I didn't. You're the only twisted one I dated." He laughed.

She smiled at him. She remembered why she had liked him so much. She felt sad at what she had done to him. "Let me go, Ayush. You don't want to do this. You'll find some other nice girl," she said, trying to appease him.

He became serious again. "No. I want to marry you. We are getting married tomorrow. Tell your parents that you prefer me to Wonderboy." He took out her cellphone. "Send prissy Wonderboy a message. Tell him you're not sure about your feelings so you've decided to go away for a few days and you want to break up with him. Tell your parents that too."

"If you call him prissy again, I'm going to hit you. And I'm not sending messages to anybody," she said stubbornly.

Fine. If you don't message him, I'll message him. I'll tell him you're dumping him because he's terrible in bed and a lousy kisser and he's not able to satisfy you," he said wickedly.

"Give me that," she exclaimed, taking the cellphone from him. She had to message her parents and Sanjay. What could she tell them? Would they believe her? It wouldn't be the first time that she had behaved irrationally. She texted Sanjay first.

"Gone away for few days to think about us," she typed as he watched. "I don't think we should be together anymore. Please cancel the wedding." She pressed the send button and composed a message to her father. She told him she was going to stay with Jayshree for a few days. "I don't want to worry them and you don't want to either. Not if you want to be their son-in-law," she said sternly.

He nodded eagerly and muttered, "Oh right. Good idea," before pressing the send button. He put the phone back into his pocket and left.

When he was gone, she searched the room again. There was an attached bathroom and several cupboards but not much else. The window in the bathroom had a strong, iron grill. One of the cupboards was full of men's clothes. She presumed they were Ayush's. The second one had a few new women's clothes with toiletries and cosmetics. He had thought about everything.

She heard the door opening. She turned and he was standing at the door looking at her. "I hope you like the clothes. I got some food. Do you want to eat here or outside, he asked.

"Outside," muttered Aditi resigned. Might as well see the

whole house, she thought. Maybe there was some place that was not secure and she could escape. They walked out of the room into a huge bedroom. It was full of his things. It suddenly hit her. She was locked in his dressing room. That explained why there were no windows. They emerged from the bedroom and entered a lavishly done up living room. She looked longingly at the front door. "Where's you're partner?" she asked casually.

"He went home. He works for my dad. And don't bother yelling or trying to escape. This is a very new building. Only the penthouse is complete. There aren't any other occupants in the building yet," He placed plastic containers of *biryani* and *raita* on the dining table and lit some candles.

"How romantic," she said sarcastically. She was surprised that she was so calm, but she didn't think Ayush would do anything to harm her. He looked too happy to see her. During dinner, he entertained her with witty stories about their common acquaintances and updated her on his life. The time passed quickly and Aditi was beginning to enjoy Ayush's company. Maybe Sanjay was right, she thought wistfully. She never gave any guy a chance. Maybe, she snorted. Sanjay was always right. He made very sure he was.

She took another serving of *biryani* and spooned some into her mouth thoughtfully. "This is a nice apartment. When did you buy this? You don't live with your parents anymore?" Aditi asked him.

"I thought you might want to live seperately after getting married. So I got this apartment done up for you. Do you like it? My construction business has really picked up. I own this entire building. I can buy you anything that you want now. What do you want, Aditi?" he asked eagerly.

Aditi became serious. Why did men keep thinking they had to buy her things to make her happy? Did she look like the materialistic sort? All she wanted was some space and freedom to be herself, which nobody wanted to give her. "I want to go home. I don't love you. You can't make someone love you. This is crazy, Ayush. Can't you see?"

Ayush closed his eyes and massaged the bridge of his nose with his fingers. A vein throbbed in his temple and his jaw tightened. "I can't live without you anymore, Aditi. If you leave me again, I'll kill myself. I swear I will. But if you give me chance, I'll do everything I can to make you happy. You loved me once. If we are together, you'll fall in love with me again."

Aditi felt a bit afraid at his sudden change of mood. She forced herself to eat another bite of *biryani* and plastered a smile on her face. "You're car is nice too. Is it new?" Ayush didn't answer. They ate the rest of their meal in silence.

After dinner, Ayush took her back to her room. He opened his cupboard and took out a T-shirt and disappeared into the bathroom. When he emerged he looked at her uncertainly. "Will you be comfortable here? You can always use my bed if you want. We can share. I won't try anything. I promise."

"No thanks. I'm fine," she said grouchily. He turned wordlessly and locked the room. Aditi began to feel teary-eyed. She wanted to sleep in her own bed not in this bed. No matter how normal Ayush might try to behave and how nicely he treated her, there was no doubt that he was psychotic and he needed help. Normal people didn't get people abducted and threathen to kill themselves. She should remember that. She used the bathroom and took off her jeans and slipped under the covers. She heard the sound of the door unlocking and Ayush walked in with a big smile on his face.

"Hello? Can't you knock?" Aditi yelled at him and pulled the covers around her. What did he want now?

"Big deal," he said grinning. "Why don't you get comfortable? Wear that nightgown I bought you. It's more comfortable."

"If you think I'm going to wear that piece of scrap, you're delusional. Now get out," she ordered feeling scared. She didn't want to give him any ideas. She shivered at the thought that she had almost slept with him before. Now he just made her skin crawl.

"Okay. I'm leaving. I just came to ask you if you need anything," he asked.

"I don't need anything," she said sadly.

"Go to sleep. I'll see you in the morning," he said softly. He went out of the room and locked the door behind him. Aditi let out a shuddering sigh of relief. She got up and locked the room from inside. Then she burst into tears.

NORMAL IS NICE

The next morning Aditi woke up early and put on her jeans. She went to the bathroom and washed her face. She tried to open the door but she couldn't. Her room had no windows so she felt disoriented. For all she knew, it was the middle of the night. She wished she atleast knew what time it was. She lay down again on the bed. Would Sanjay believe her text, she wondered. It was possible. Anybody who knew her would believe her text. She has a history of being irresponsible and flighty. She drifted off to sleep again.

Aditi woke up when she heard a knock on the door. "Come have tea, Aditi," said Ayush.

Aditi got up and followed Ayush into his bedroom. She sat on an armchair next to the coffee table on which two cups of tea were placed.

He looked at her assessingly. "You've changed, you know that? Nobody would have caught you dead in this boring T-shirt and jeans before you met Wonderboy. You used to dress up so glamorously, Aditi. Wonderboy doesn't like it when you wear sexy clothes, does he? He prefers it when you dress like a

219

plain little sparrow. He doesn't want other people to find you attractive. I can actually sympathize with him, but I'll never ask you to change for me, Aditi." he said amused.

Aditi stared at him with disbelief. He was holding her against her will and forcing her to marry him and he had the gall to claim that he would never ask her to change. She knew that there was no point in arguing with him. "Stop calling him Wonderboy. His name is Sanjay and he doesn't like nicknames," she said sulkily. Some of Ayush's words rang true. She didn't really care what she wore nowadays but not because Sanjay didn't approve of her clothes. It didn't make sense to wear her expensive designer clothes when she was with Sanjay. She couldn't take the risk of Sanjay's impatient hands ruining any of her precious clothes. They were just going to wind up on the floor at the end of the night anyway. She smiled dreamily.

She snapped out of her day-dreaming and turned to Ayush. "I don't understand why are you punishing Sanjay? He has not done anything to hurt you. You're angry at me but you're making me do the same thing to him that I did to you. Think about how you felt, Ayush. Why do you want him to go through the same thing?"

Ayush felt silent. "Why should I care what he feels?" he growled. He leaned back against his chair and stared off into space. Finally, he got up and stalked out of the room.

Aditi looked around the room. When he wasn't back after five minutes, she tentatively made her way out of the room. He was not in the living room. She made her way to the front door and turned the knob of the front door with trembling hands. It was unlocked. Aditi stared at it with surprise. She was just about to step out when Ayush's suicide threats echoed in her head. The house was eerily quiet. She stood at the entrance uncertainly. She sighed and made her way back and searched the house. Ayush was sitting on the floor of the kitchen and staring blankly into space.

She knelt next to him and put her arms around him. "I'm so sorry. I'm really, really sorry. If there is anything I could do to change this, I would. You need help, Ayush. This is not normal."

"Why didn't you leave?" he asked, avoiding her gaze.

"I couldn't leave you like this." She sat cross-legged next to him. "You'll find someone one day, Ayush. I know it feels horrible now but everything will pass. One day, you'll look back on this day and laugh."

"Your purse is in that cupboard. Go," he said quietly, not looking at her. Aditi walked to the cupboard and retrieved her purse. She called Sanjay and put her phone back into her purse.

"Come on. You can't sit on the floor like this," she scolded sternly and pulled him up. He stood up and stalked to the bedroom and banged the door behind him.

Half an hour later, the doorbell rang and Aditi went to answer the door. Sanjay walked inside distraught. He pulled Aditi into his arms and buried his face in her hair. "Adi. Oh Adi. From the moment I got your text I knew something was horribly wrong. We've been searching for you all night. And then your parents called and said you were at Mayank's when I knew you were not. I just lost my mind. I'm not going to let you go anywhere alone. I'm so sorry for letting you go alone," he murmured over and over.

Aditi pulled away from him surprised. "You didn't believe the text? Then you do trust me." Delight spread deliciously through her body.

Sanjay looked puzzled. "Of course I trust you. It's the guys I don't trust. Why would I believe such a ridiculous message?"

"Well thank God for that," said Aditi fervently.

Mayank and his brother, Jayant walked into the house. They looked tired and worn and stared at her with concern. "Are you okay, Aditi? Did he hurt you? If he did, we can go kill him now. Where is he?" said Mayank vehemently. Aditi motioned towards the bedroom.

"We had almost found you when you called. We phoned all your friends and then all your ex-boyfriends. Atleast the ones we knew about. Ayush was the only one who was not picking up his phone. We got in touch with his parents and they said he hadn't contacted them in a week. His parents are worried too. They are going to be here any minute," said Sanjay. "Then Vishal got in touch with his DSP friend and they tracked your cellphone. I should have done that first. I don't know why I didn't think about it. My only excuse was that I was crazy with worry."

"Vishal? Vishal, my ex-boyfriend? You met all my exes?" Aditi cringed with embarrassment. Jealous, possessive Sanjay had spoken to all her ex-boyfriends. She felt a little queasy. What must he think of her? She sat down on the bed and imagined the scene. "You did that for me?"

"Yeah. It wasn't so bad," he said wryly, sitting on the sofa next to her. "All of them have suprisingly fond memories of you. Some of them even offered to help. Vishal seemed to think that I was suffering from cancer. I don't know why? Would you know something about that, Adi?" Sanjay eyes crinkled with amusement.

"I don't know why he would get such a silly idea," she muttered. "I'm so sorry, Sanjay. For all this mess."

"Nonsense. You can't blame this on yourself. This guy has issues. We went through tough times and got out, didn't we? He'll do the same. I can understand why he would want to lock you up in the house though. I feel like doing it myself sometimes. What were you thinking when you were strolling in such a deserted area at night all by yourself?" he scolded.

"I was doing the wedding shopping," she explained. "You really spoke to all my exes?"

"Yeah. You know, I get it now. You have to kiss a few frogs to find your prince. All those guys I met..." He shook his head. "They were so wrong for you."

"Oh. And who's right for me?" she asked teasingly.

"Sharad. You two are like Ken and Barbie. Luckily for me, the two of you don't want to be together," he replied seriously and she hit him.

Aditi suddenly remembered her parents. "My parents. They must be so worried. I should call them."

"No need. Jayshree told them you were with her. We didn't want to worry them unnecessarily, but you can call them if you want."

Sharad walked in just as Mayank stepped out to call Jayshree and tell her about the recent developments. He grabbed her and hugged her tight. "Thank God you're safe. We were all going crazy." He kissed her on both cheeks. Aditi glaced anxiously at Sanjay but he was just looking tired and relieved. Aditi felt tears run down her cheeks. "You guys are the greatest. I didn't realise I had such good friends," she said tremulously.

Mayank walked in. "Ayush's parents are here. We can leave." He hesitated. "The police wanted to know if you're going to press charges, Aditi." Aditi looked up to see the small group that entered the house and disappeared into the bedroom.

"I don't want to press charges, Sanjay. I just want to forget this whole thing. He might be a little crazy but he didn't do anything to hurt me. I can't ruin his whole future because of it. I just want to go home and sip a cup of strong coffee," she said tiredly.

Mayank and Sharad turned to Sanjay. "Is she serious? You're just going to let this go? You should file an FIR. The bastard should go to jail," said Sharad ferociously.

Sanjay shrugged. "I'm just glad we found her. It's upto Aditi. Whatever she's comfortable with. If we blow this out-of-proportion, it'll simply be all over the papers tomorrow. I don't want to overreact." Sanjay smiled at Aditi gently.

"We have to call everybody and tell them she's fine. I'm going to call Vishal," muttered Mayank.

Aditi linked her arm through Sanjay's. "I just want to go home now."

"Which home, Adi? Do you want to go with Mayank, or to your parent's place or with me?" said Sanjay pulling her into his arms.

"Home. Our home. There's no other home." She slipped her hand in his and squeezed. He winced. She looked at his hand. It was raw and bleeding mildly. "What happened to your hand?" she asked concerned.

"I punched Nikhil when I went to his place to search for you. His teeth cut into my knuckles. I should have aimed for his nose," he replied thoughtfully.

"You went to Nikhil's house and punched him?" she exclaimed in horror. She couldn't picture Sanjay punching anybody. "And you're claiming you're not going to overreact? What do you call this?"

"Hey. He deserved it. He was saying something stupid about you in front of his wife and I'm allowed to defend your honour," said Sanjay self-righteously. "Anyway, I was going to hit him one of these days. He's such a dickhead."

"I was wondering how you're sitting here so calmly with everything going on," she scolded him. "We'll discuss this later. Right now, I'm just glad it's over."

"Me too, Adi. I so glad you're safe," said Sanjay.

She smiled at him. Sometimes, normal was just what you needed.